SHE A BADDIE

MONIQUE FISHER

SHE A BADDIE

CHRISTOPHER

Christopher Rossmore sits in his office reviewing all the praise Rossmore Wineries received from Senator Greg Kelly and his wife Tiana. Their anniversary party went off without a hitch. The Kellys and their guests have been raving about it on social media over the past two days.

There's a knock on his door. Chris looks up and in walks Paula, his co-executive director of the private events department.

"Did you see all the tweets?" She smiles.

"I'm reading them now," Chris replies. "We really pulled it off."

"Yes, we did."

"I couldn't have done any of this without you, Paula."

"I know," She jokes. The two share a laugh. "You just remember that when you become CEO, Mr. Rossmore."

"Don't worry. I will *not* forget you. That VP position is as good as yours."

"Thank you kindly. Speaking of which, when are you meeting with your dad?"

Chris checks his watch. "The meeting is in twenty minutes, but I'll head there now. After all, being on time means being late."

"You are just like Sam," Paula smiles wistfully.

"Thank you."

"We really miss him around here."

"So do I."

"You better get going."

"Right. Get ready to move into a bigger office."

Chris heads to his father Blake Rossmore's office. This morning Chris received an email from Blake to meet with him to discuss something of "great importance." It can only mean one thing—Chris is about to be made CEO of Rossmore Wineries.

The butterflies in his stomach flutter. He's been waiting for this moment his whole life. For as long as he can remember, his late grandfather, Samuel Rossmore, wanted him to become CEO. And that day has finally arrived. Chris currently works as the executive director of private events. Grandpa Sam thought it was important for Chris to hone his skills working at the winery's main office. Chris started as an intern in college and worked his way up to his current position over the course of ten years. Between that time, and spending most of his adolescence with his grandpa around vineyards, Chris knows all there is to know about the wine business.

When he approaches his father's office, Chris takes a deep breath. "Don't let him see your nerves. You've earned this." He knocks in three quick taps.

"Come in, Christopher," His father calls out.

Chris opens the door and is surprised to see Trinese, his father's fiancée, standing to the side of the entry. She smiles at Chris, but the smile doesn't reach her eyes. It never does. Their interactions can best be described as tolerable but not friendly. She's going to be Chris' fifth stepmother and she's only four years older than him. Chris knows that if he wants to have a relationship with his father, Trinese comes with the package. Still, it's not something he likes.

"Hello, Trinese," Chris says, trying his best to sound affable.

"Hello, Chris," Trinese replies with a smirk and eyeballs him like she's sizing up an opponent.

Chris has dealt with this before. All of his former stepmothers saw him as competition for his father's affection at first, but they needn't have worried. Blake never took to fatherhood like most dads. It wasn't until he got sick ten years ago that he seemed to decide that ignoring his only child may not be the best move.

Eventually, Chris and Blake formed somewhat of a close bond but when Grandpa Sam died, that bond was put to the test. Sadly, Blake started reverting to his former self, and him getting engaged to Trinese just made things worse. Chris holds out hope that he and his father can make their way back to each other.

"Chris, take a seat." Blake gestures to the chair across his desk.

Feeling like a kid who got sent to the principal's office, Chris sits down doing his best to brush aside nervous energy before he speaks.

"Before you say anything"—Chris takes another breath—"I want you to know that I don't take this responsibility lightly. I will make you and Grandpa Sam proud when I take over."

"Yeah, about that. Chris, during my tenure as CEO it's become apparent that you don't have what it takes to make Rossmore into the brand it needs to be."

Wait, what?

"Rossmore needs someone with their finger on the pulse of consumers; someone who will engage with people and take this company to new heights. That's why Trinese will take over when I step down this summer."

Chris' eye twitches. The room sways causing him to feel like he's either going to faint or vomit.

This cannot be happening.

"Is this a joke?" Chris asks.

"I assure you it's not. Don't worry, your position in private events is still safe," Blake replies brusquely.

"But I've been working at the winery's main office for ten years. This is my birthright! The job should go to me," Chris says trying to keep his voice even because he knows getting emotional won't make Blake listen to him.

"Chris, you have done well, but I think it's time we go in a new direction." Blake looks lovingly at Trinese. The victorious look she gave Chris earlier all makes sense now.

"Dad… Senior Rossmore, my contributions have increased revenue for the company by over twenty-five percent. I have brought in more business than any of my predecessors, and my idea to partner with local farm-to-table restaurants for the monthly wine tastings has been nothing but a success. Hell, Senator Kelly is raving about us online as we speak."

"You're right, Chris. The private events department has thrived with you and Paula at the helm. The partnership you two cultivated has been tremendous. But I have to go with the decision I think is best for the company. And with Trinese's ability to connect with people, I think she'll excel as CEO."

"I connect with people," Chris argued.

They laugh. *They actually have the nerve to fucking laugh.*

"Chris, figures and number crunching are your thing. It's why Paula is in charge of handling all the clients."

Fuck. He has a point. Being a people person has always been a challenge. His grandfather gave him more than enough chances to show his acumen for presentations, and it went badly each time. Chris cringes at the thought.

"Chris," Trinese interjects disrupting his thoughts. "I truly believe I have what's required to take Rossmore to the next level. I think outside the box and Blake recognizes that. I hope that you and I can work well together. I promise I will be a fair and patient boss."

Chris looks at his father's flavor of the month. "I have a degree in finance, not to mention an MBA in business analytics. Trinese… you don't. You're a college dropout who can't keep a job. How exactly does that qualify you to do… anything?"

"I have plenty of customer service and hospitality experience, Christopher. And I don't appreciate you questioning my abilities," Trinese sneered.

"You don't have any!" Chris shot back.

Blake jumps in. "Alright, that's enough you two. I'll tell you what, I have an idea. Michaela Hamilton and Hunter Lawrence just announced their engagement. The wedding is in May and I plan to hand over the reins in June. This will no doubt be a lavish affair. It will also serve as a test for both of you. Whichever one of you books them as a client, becomes CEO."

"That's a fool's errand. Are you forgetting that Parker Hamilton always insists his kids have their weddings at the family ranch?" Chris argues. "As long as he's paying, Michaela will be getting married there too."

"I have it on good authority that Michaela has

convinced her father to let her and Hunter have the wedding somewhere else," Blake retorts.

"How good of an authority?" Chris asks.

"Parker told me himself." Blake grins. "So, what do you say?"

Fuck! Blake knows egging Chris on will work. Chris has always been naturally competitive, and booking a Hamilton wedding for Rossmore Wineries would be a huge win. A Hamilton has never gotten married anywhere besides their family property since they acquired it fifteen years ago. The Hamiltons are Black American royalty. The patriarch of the family owns a media conglomerate of radio stations, television, magazines, and news programs. Hosting a family of that caliber would open up Rossmore to a whole new level of clientele, and make it a premiere wedding venue. They're doing well now, but booking this wedding will be a game changer. And the challenge of convincing Michaela—who is basically a female version of her dad, intimidating and a straight shooter—has Chris intrigued and a little nervous... okay terrified, but there's no way he's backing down.

"I'm game," Trinese beams confidently.

"So, what do you say Chris? May the best candidate win?" Blake holds out his hand for Chris to shake it.

Chris looks at his father's hand, feeling like he's about to make a deal with the devil.

This is a mistake. Senior Rossmore is definitely going to make me regret this, but what choice do I have? I can't just sit back and watch all that my grandfather built go up in smoke.

Chris shakes his father's hand as a chill runs down his spine.

"Alright. You have a deal."

2

CHRISTOPHER

It's been two days since Chris' meeting with his dad and Trinese. He's still in disbelief that Trinese is what's standing in his way to becoming CEO. This woman met his dad as a flight attendant last year on his way to Paris. She got fired for missing too many days soon after. The next thing Chris knows, she's at the office practically every day.

Chris has felt his father's love slipping away for a while now. He wasn't even surprised when they got engaged, but this? This he couldn't have foreseen. It's probably the most hurtful thing his father has ever done to him.

Pushing away all thoughts of his crumbling life, Chris focuses his attention on Izzie. Izzie is Chris' best friend who's back after three years of traveling around the globe with her father Lyman as they built their family's business brand. Izzie is set to take over as CEO of Taylor Made Haircare, a company her father started twenty-three years ago. She's going to meet with Taylor Made's board of directors in a few weeks for the official vote. There's no doubt she has it in the bag. Izzie is the type of baddie who walks into a room and everything stops. In other words, the opposite of Chris. He still sometimes can't believe Isobel Brooke Taylor, a ray of sunshine, is his closest friend.

Tonight, Chris and the crew are meeting at LW, Izzie's favorite restaurant, for a welcome home dinner. She flew in from Trinidad a few days ago but Chris, Artie, Freddie, and Heather agreed to give Izzie a few days to get settled before bombarding her with how much they missed her. Especially Chris. He really missed Izzie. And knowing she was home but not being able to see her has been torture. This is the longest the two have gone without seeing each other. They've always been each other's constant companion. She's the sun and he's her shade.

Chris pulls up to valet parking and hands the attendant the keys to his Porsche Cayenne. It's a congratulatory gift from his grandfather he got after Chris and Paula booked the wedding for Katie

Patterson, the granddaughter of Shoe Shine Records CEO TK Patterson. It is Rossmore's biggest event to date—that is until Michaela and Hunter have their wedding through the family business.

The Sonoma location would be perfect for them. Their guest list will no doubt be huge.

Chris hands the attendant a hundred bucks and heads inside. He doesn't even know why he's entertaining the idea of pitching to Michaela and Hunter. Paula's a pro, but he can't rely on her outgoing personality during *his* presentation. Going to her for help wouldn't work. Besides, he doesn't trust his competition. For all he knows, Trinese has already gotten to Paula. Not that he thinks Paula would sell him out, but he also didn't think his father would either. Look how that turned out.

The very thought of giving a presentation to Michaela and Hunter fills him with dread. The last time Chris gave a presentation, he fumbled his words so badly that Paula had to step in. And the worst part? It happened in front of his grandfather *and* his father. It's no wonder his dad doesn't think he can do it.

Chris enters the restaurant and finds his friends sans Izzie. He smiles. No doubt she's planning to be fashionably late and make an entrance. Heather sees him first and smiles as she gets up to hug him. In that second, all worries of work melt away. He loves these people like family. Being in their presence always makes him feel cared for and appreciated. Chris hugs Heather tightly. Heather is a spoiled rich girl with a heart of gold. She's also a daddy's girl who could convince the man to buy her the moon. Case in point, between her outfit, jewelry, hair, makeup, and shoes, she's easily wearing close to forty thousand dollars. But as coddled as she is, at her core, Heather is caring and will do anything for those she loves. She and Izzie were Chris's lifeline in high school. Next, he hugs Artie, they became friends in college and have been tight ever since. He became part of the crew shortly after. And last, is Freddie. Chris and Freddie became friends when Izzie brought him into the fold after she saw his act at the Kitten Heel Cabaret. Freddie is a female impersonator known for his Chantel Stone persona. Watching Freddie perform tricks your mind into thinking you're actually seeing the R&B superstar.

Freddie retakes his seat and to no one's surprise, he and Artie are seated together with their hands touching each other's thighs. The two have mutual crushes on each other but neither will act on it much to everyone else's chagrin. The reason being that

Artie is deep in his ho phase and Freddie has no interest in being one of his regulars.

"Look at you, Mr. Rossmore!" Freddie gushes.

"What?" Chris asks.

"Oh, c'mon, Chris, you're in a suit," Artie replies.

"I wear suits all the time," Chris argues as he takes a seat.

He notices his friends leave two seats open right next to each other for him and Izzie. Ever since Izzie rescued him that day in high school, they have always sat next to each other. Somethings never change, no matter how much time has passed.

Chris sees this and smiles.

"You didn't honestly think any of us would be foolish enough to separate you and the Duchess, did you?" Heather says reading his mind.

"I would hope not," Chris jokes.

"But seriously, Chris, you usually wear business suits. You look like you're about to hit the club," Freddie says. "And did you get a fresh line up, too?"

"I mean, we are about to be graced by the presence of Isobel Taylor." Chris grins. "I couldn't come half stepping."

"I know that's right," A voice behind him says.

Chris turns and is greeted by Izzie's beautiful smile. *Sunshine.* As usual, Ms. Taylor comes looking like the life of the party. She is dressed in a figure-hugging emerald green, velvet, long sleeve bodycon dress. She has on minimal make up, just a simple glossed lip with some liner and mascara. And with her hair bone straight, parted down the middle, Izzie is breathtaking, to say the least. She's beyond gorgeous. Chris' smile grows a mile wide. Her smile is just as big. Without a moment left to spare, Izzie flies into Chris' arms. They hold each other so tightly that folks around them applaud.

When they finally decide to break apart, they playfully bow to their adoring public who are all captivated by Izzie. She just has a way about her where people immediately love her. The only time Chris isn't timid is when he's in her presence. That's the power of Izzie.

He guides her to their table and friends, and she hugs all of them before taking her seat. The server arrives within seconds.

"Hello, Ms. Taylor, and welcome back. Would you like the usual?" The server asks.

"Oh, you're new! Where's Katie?" Izzie replies with a toothy grin.

"Katie got promoted and is now the manager at the LW in Culver City."

"Good for her. And yes, thank you…" Izzie leans in to read her name tag. "Irene."

"Thank you, and what can I get everyone else to drink?"

The crew gives Irene their drink orders and she swiftly exits making her way toward the bar.

"So, how was Trinidad?" Chris asks. "We didn't talk much while you were there."

"Chris, what's wrong?" Izzie asks.

"What? Nothing," Chris replies confused.

"Chris, it's me. I can tell when something is off about you. What's wrong?"

"Iz, I don't want to—"

"Christopher Samuel Rossmore." She has one eyebrow raised and a smirk knowingly plastered across her face.

She knows those are the three magic words to get me to say anything.

"My dad wants to make Trinese CEO," Chris confesses.

There's a long silence from all of his friends.

"CEO of what?" Artie finally asks.

"Rossmore Wineries," Chris answers.

Irene comes back with their drinks. She sets them down and gives an awkward smile as everyone stares at Chris, their mouths wide open.

Everyone takes a sip from their drinks except Chris. He finishes his in one gulp before signaling Irene to come back. She sets down another vodka soda within minutes.

"You should probably keep them coming, Irene," Artie says.

She nods in understanding.

Chris sips his drink.

"Chris, we get why you're drinking but slow down," Heather says. "We haven't eaten anything yet."

Chris nabs a piece of bread from the basket on the table and bites into it.

Izzie is quiet. Really quiet.

Curious, Chris starts, hoping she'll have some words of encouragement. "Iz—"

"I'm going to murder your father," Izzie declares.

Irene sets Chris' third drink down looking at Izzie with concern.

"Relax, Irene," Freddie smiles. "She's not actually going to murder anyone."

"Oh, no. I am. But not you sweetie," Izzie says to Irene.

"I heard the part about his dad. Frankly, I'm more concerned with you getting caught. Mr. Rossmore and his fiancée were here last week, and he didn't even tip me. So, murder away," Irene replies. "Now what can I get you?"

"We'll have the chef's tasting menu," Artie says.

"Sounds good." Irene writes down their order and exits.

Izzie points to Irene as she walks away. "You see! Nobody cares. Blake Rossmore won't be missed and I'm rich. I can totally get away with it."

"You seem to be forgetting you're also a Black woman who lives in America," Artie says.

"Fine, but if there is anything I can do let me know," Izzie tells Chris.

"You can try and get me connected with Michaela Hamilton. She and Hunter Lawrence are getting married. Blake has decided to make booking them a test for both me and Trinese. Whoever wins gets the job."

"That's ridiculous," Heather says. "Isn't she a flight attendant?"

"Not since she and Blake got together. She got fired, remember?" Chris reminds Heather.

"So, she's going from flight attendant to CEO if she wins?" Freddie asks. "She must have sucked and fucked Blake real good to force that decision from him."

"Fred, please." Chris holds his stomach.

"That's not from what I said. It's from the vodka, young man," Freddie asserts.

"Still though." Chris sips his water.

When Chris looks over at Izzie, she's typing away on her phone.

"Iz, what are you doing?"

"I checked Michaela's IG and it seems her and some friends are having a couples retreat at Hamilton ranch in two weeks. She and I used to be pretty tight—"

"Yeah, what happened? After she moved to Europe, she kind of just fell off the face of the Earth," Heather says. "I've only heard about her through the vultures at TRNN."

"You just answered your own question. The assholes at The Rich Nigga Network became so relentless that she dipped. Pretty soon, it was impossible to keep in contact with her," Izzie answers still pecking away at her screen. "I'm sending her a quick note so Chris and I can go to the retreat."

"But you and Chris aren't a couple," Artie says.

"We are now," Izzie smiles.

Chris could kiss Izzie. Of course, she uses her power of knowing everyone to help him. He was so shocked and dismayed by his father's decision, it didn't even occur to him to look to Izzie for help. He was too focused on how much he missed her. Chris reminds himself not to get too excited. Getting ahold of Michaela may be more of a challenge than he knows. She's notorious for not taking disruptions lightly, hence her hatred of TRNN. Chris can't believe The Rich Nigga Network is their actual name. They have been hounding Michaela and her family forever. They are a group of media vultures that prey on rich and famous Black folks for gossip that's mostly untrue.

"How long is the retreat?" Heather asks.

"Five days," Izzie answers. "It's starts on the twenty-eighth and ends on the third."

"You think Michaela will be okay with us attending?" Chris asks.

Just then, Izzie's phone buzzes. She reads the message, smiles then shows Chris.

MICHAELA

Hey Izzie! Long time no see. I know I've been MIA but you know how the parasites at TRNN are—

Izzie most definitely understands. The only person who got more attention than Michaela was her. Even being away for three years didn't stop them from going after Izzie.

MICHAELA

Of course you can come. We have a
lot to catch up on. And you're with
Chris Rossmore? I have to admit, I
never would have put you two
together—

Gee, thanks Michaela.

MICHAELA

It's going to be a fun retreat. Can't
wait to see you both there.

Chris bypasses Michaela's small dig and hugs Izzie. While this helps him get close to the happy couple, Chris still has to worry about his pitch, but for now he's celebrating this win.

When Irene comes back with their food, Izzie orders a bottle of champagne.

The crew talks, drinks, laughs, and eats.

Engulfed by triumph, Chris takes Izzie's hand catching her gaze.

"Thank you," he says softly.

"Of course, Chris," She smiles. "Don't worry, that job is as good as yours."

Let's hope. He smiles back and kisses her hand.

3

ISOBEL

I zzie wakes up with a hangover. She feels like a block of cement. Her throat is dry, and her head is pounding. She examines the room, and nothing looks familiar. It is then she realizes she isn't in a deluxe suite at the Park-Barrington in Trinidad anymore, she's back home, just not her home. She's in the main bedroom of Chris' condo.

She sits up, thanking God her meeting with the board members of Taylor Made isn't today. If it was she'd be in deep shit.

The night before slowly trickles into her memory. Ah, yes! She and Chris are a couple. At least for the time being. They just need to get him that promotion.

God, Blake Rossmore is a real piece of shit.

Izzie knew that "I'm sick and ready to be a father" schtick he had going wouldn't last. She anxiously waited for the other shoe to drop but she didn't imagine it would happen like this. That man makes Satan look like Jesus. Izzie would never say this to Chris' face, but moments like this make her even happier and more grateful to have a father who trusts her and knows what she's capable of. Chris used to have someone like that in his life, but Grandpa Sam died six months ago. Izzie feels an overwhelming sense of guilt for not making it to the funeral. Her schedule wouldn't allow it. Still, she can't help but think that if she had been there to console Chris all this shit wouldn't be piling up on him.

Making her way across the room, Izzie notices her dress slung over Chris' desk chair. She's wearing an oversized t-shirt and boxers. Her hair is wrapped, and a bonnet is on her head.

Chris.

She smiles. As tipsy as he was, he still made sure she was taken care of. That's Chris in a nutshell, he always puts others before himself. His exes could never appreciate that quality which is why they all sucked. The thought of Chris with another woman causes a surge of jealousy to course through Izzie.

Her unconscious must think that she and Chris are a real couple because she's never felt anything like this before. Not liking anyone he dated is one thing, this is something altogether different. Her disapproval of his exes came from a place of protection. Chris has always been kind-hearted and mild mannered. The type that can be easily taken advantage of. Izzie took it upon herself to make sure he wasn't used by any gold-digging skanks, convincing him to dismiss them at the first whiff of deception. Coming back to reality, Izzie shakes her head—she needs to keep that shit in check.

In the kitchen, Izzie grabs two bottles of water and wanders around the house in search of the guest room Chris fell asleep in. Down the hall, she could hear the ceiling fan whirling. *He must be in there.* And that's where she finds him; sprawled on the bed, passed out on top of the covers in just his draws with his glasses still on.

Izzie giggles and thinks back to how she and Chris first met. They were fifteen and attended the same high school, Blythe-Wood Academy, a predominantly Black school for the wealthy. Chris was new and was being bullied constantly. It was hard to witness. Izzie couldn't take seeing this poor kid get treated like shit, especially since he was really smart and sweet. They shared a few classes and one day Izzie approached the lunch table where Chris was sitting. As usual, he was being hassled when she asked him to sit with her and Heather. Later, Chris told her that he knew she was only being nice out of pity, but also that he didn't care if she was. Folks at school said it was like watching Lisa Turtle—Izzie—and Hilary Banks—Heather—become friends with Steve Urkel. And lucky for Chris, Izzie and Heather, especially Izzie, couldn't care less what everyone else thinks. Besides, she had so much cachet that she could afford to become friends with a lesser-known student, all it did was make Chris popular.

"Are you staring at me, Sunflower?" Chris mumbles still half asleep.

Izzie laughs. Chris has called her that since their school trip to Half Moon Bay. Izzie was enamored with the sunflower fields to such an extent that they almost missed the bus. She in turn calls him Tiger like his favorite superhero Spider-Man is called by Mary Jane Watson.

"I was just waiting for you to wake up so I could give you some water, Tiger."

Chris rolls over onto his back and leans up. Izzie notices his six-pack. He was a late bloomer and didn't start to gain muscle until he was at least twenty-one. When that happened, he hit the gym like a demon. She spies his happy trail and feels flushed. Her pussy pulsates at the idea of seeing what's beneath the waistband of his boxers.

What the hell? This is Chris. My best friend. What is happening?

Izzie shakes it off by making a joke. "You've been built like a super-hero for seven years and I still can't get over it."

"That's because you've known me since I was a string bean." Chris gets out of bed and takes a bottle of water from her.

He grabs a t-shirt from his dresser and gulps the water before he lies back down.

"How did you manage to get me out of my dress and into your clothes?" Izzie asks.

"Easy. Your back was turned to me, so I unzipped your dress and pulled the t-shirt over your head. Believe it or not, you actually put my draws on yourself."

"I have a vague memory of that. So, you didn't see my goods?"

"Nope. I did not."

Why am I disappointed?

"You want to get breakfast?" Izzie asks, still

attempting to move past her sudden attraction to Chris.

The simple fact is that Chris is fine. Always has been. And we're talking Kofi Siriboe levels of fine, but they're friends. Izzie coupling up with him is purely a favor. Besides, she's focused on making the move to CEO herself. Getting involved with anyone isn't in the cards.

"Do I have to get back up?" Chris asks.

"Yes, Chris. You do."

"Give me a minute."

A minute turns into an hour. The good news is that they both spend so much time at one another's places that they each have clothes. A few of their respective exes had a problem with that. Hell, most of them had a problem with Izzie and Chris' friendship period. But they're all being paid dust because there was no way Izzie and Chris were going to stop being friends over someone else's insecurity.

Chris drives them to a diner they both love in Eagle Rock. He has pancakes and she has an omelet.

"So, I was thinking if we're going to do this boyfriend/girlfriend thing we need to get to know each other," Izzie proposes.

"Izzie, we've known each other for thirteen years." Chris pours syrup on his pancakes.

"Yeah, as friends. We don't know a lot of intimate stuff about each other."

"We know plenty. You've seen me with my exes and I've seen you with yours."

"That's not the same, Chris, and you know it."

He offers her a bite of his pancakes. She takes it.

"Mmm. That's good."

"Yep, can't go wrong with pecan." He smiles and winks before taking a bite.

Oh, my God! I wish I was that fork. Damnit, Isobel, stop it. Relax, you're just horny. It has been a minute.

All the traveling didn't leave a lot of time for romance. Heather is always telling Izzie that she needs to have a designated dick on standby like her. Izzie wonders if Chris would be open to that thanks to their new arrangement.

She clears her throat and chuckles. "Seriously though, we should present ourselves as a couple."

"Okay, how do you mean?"

"We should kiss," Izzie suggests.

This isn't because I want to kiss Chris' soft pillowy lips. It's for the cause. That's it!

Chris' eyes grow wide. "Now?"

"Why not?"

He sips his orange juice, puts the glass down, and slides over to her side of the booth. They look at each other with nervous trepidation. Just when Izzie is about to tell Chris that he doesn't have to do this, he takes her face in his hands, leans in, and places his lips on hers. His tongue slides along hers in a kiss that sends a shock to Izzie's system.

Oh, dear God. This was a mistake.

Their arms wrap around each other as if it's always been their rightful place. Izzie kisses Chris along his jawline, licking and taking bites.

"Mmmm, Izzie." He moans.

"Fuck, Chris." She backs away. "We should stop."

"Right."

They reconnect and kiss until both of their phones buzz at the same time. The two break apart and stare into each other's eyes until Izzie's phone buzzes again followed by Chris'.

It was odd for both their phones to go off at the same time. Something must be going on. They pick up their phones and unlock the screens where they both find messages from Artie. He's sent each of them an article from TRNN.

Chris Rossmore as Izzie Taylor's Knight in Shining Armor?! See the photos inside.

They scroll through the images and see Chris

holding his arm out so an overzealous photographer can't get closer to Izzie while his other arm is around her.

"Do you remember that?" Izzie asks.

"Kind of," Chris replies.

Artie sends them a text.

ARTIE

Did you two see the pics and the article?

IZZIE

Pics, yes. The article, not yet.

ARTIE

Read it!

Christopher Rossmore, heir to the Rossmore Wineries fortune was seen holding Izzie Taylor, heiress to the Taylor Made Haircare fortune and socialite. When our TRNN photog tried to snap a picture of the Duchess, Mr. Rossmore wasn't having it, telling our guy to "back off."

The two have been friends for years, but from the looks of things, friendship isn't the only thing going on between them! Izzie has dated everyone from athletes to actors. This is a turn we didn't see coming as Rossmore is not well known for his presence on red carpets.

What do ya'll think? Can these friends to lovers go the distance? Or should Izzie go back to her tried and true pretty boys?

ARTIE
It looks like the couple thing is
already working.

Izzie looks at the tight protective hold Chris has on her and the expression on his face. He looked pissed. Izzie has her arms around Chris, not unlike when they just kissed. The comments section is going crazy.

"He's fine as hell. Where he been?"
"You see them titties? I know he sucking on them all day. Shit, I would."
"I bet his dick is huge."

Great. Now I'm thinking about Chris' dick. Thanks, random commenter.

"Izzie a bad bitch but she can do better."

"Fuck you!" Chris responds.

"Ignore it, Chris," Izzie laughs.

"I swear I don't know how you handle this. My family's business has been around longer than yours. How come they never come after me? They only bother you and, on occasion, Heather."

"You read the article. You never go anywhere," Izzie teases.

"I go places," Chris playfully argues.

"Somewhere besides comic bookstores, Chris."

"Oh, speaking of which—"

"You ready to hit up Elite Power?" Izzie asks.

"Only if you are," Chris grins.

"Let's do it."

They enter Elite Power, a Black owned comic bookstore that sells everything but caters to indie Black works. Chris goes straight to the Marvel section to pick up the latest edition of Miles Morales while Izzie checks out an indie piece by Wyvetta Pierce. It's called *Nightshade*. Izzie loves it. It's about a group of nomads, each with a unique superpower, that travel the world righting wrongs—and they're all Black women. Word is that a show is being developed by the streaming service Echo and Izzie can't wait.

She chuckles at how Chris got her so deeply into

comic books. When they met, Izzie purely read romance novels and Vogue. They had only been friends for a few weeks when he first took her to a comic bookstore. When he suggested it, she thought he was joking.

Chris slides up next to her and reads over her shoulder. "Who do you think should play Shelby?"

"Jamila Hawkins, of course." Izzie turns to face him. "Chris, I have a question for you."

"Ask away."

Alright, here goes.

"What's your favorite sexual position?"

"Damn, you're really going all in," Chris chuckles.

"You should be, too."

"I know, but c'mon, Iz, this is a little weird. We've never talked about this type of stuff before, now it's suddenly being thrust at us. This doesn't make you feel a little weird, too?"

Izzie understands where Chris is coming from. The basis of their friendship has been them looking out for each other. This unexpected attraction could complicate things, but it's too late now. They have to go through with this.

"Yeah, but it's something a couple would know about each other, and we have two weeks until the retreat. You want to pull this off, don't you?"

"Of course." Chris pushes his glasses up the bridge of his nose. "It's missionary."

"Why?" Izzie tries not to sound disappointed.

She reminds herself that she and Chris will not be having sex, but she was hoping for a more interesting answer. Missionary to her is basically the vanilla ice cream of sex. It's good but there's better flavors.

Chris shrugs. "I like seeing the look on a woman's face when she comes."

Izzie feels her panties get moist at Chris' words.

Holy shit! This is going to be a long ass few weeks.

4

ISOBEL

Later that week, they are walking hand-in-hand as they browse the farmer's market when fresh cod catches Izzie's attention.

"What do you say to fish and chips for dinner?" Izzie asks.

It's interesting being out with Chris as his "girl-friend," when a lot of the stuff they've been doing isn't any different from before she was gone. They've gone to bookstores, shopping, and eating the best dishes at their favorite restaurants. It's like they're just doing regular friendship things, but now that they need to present themselves as a couple, every-thing they do is cloaked in their new relationship; and frankly it's driving Izzie a little crazy. It's like her heart, brain, and pussy were in direct conflict.

Her pussy wants to fuck Chris, her heart wants to make him hers, and her brain is telling them both to shut the fuck up.

"Sounds good to me. You want me to help?"

"That works."

While Izzie makes more than enough money to hire a cook, she enjoys cooking for herself. Cleaning is a different story. She happily relies on a housekeeping service that sends a maid three times a week. They have all signed NDAs, so she knows no one has ever sold her out to TRNN.

Speak of the devil.

"Izzie! Chris! Over here!" a guy with a camera calls out to them.

"Shit," Izzie says.

"Just ignore him."

"Easier said than done, Chris."

The photographer gets closer. "Let's get a kiss!"

Before Izzie can say anything, Chris pulls her close and lays one on her that's even better than the instance at the diner. When they break apart, they're staring at each other again. This time, Izzie bites her lip, wondering how good of a kisser Chris is of lower lips.

"We're good." Chris tells the photographer.

Right, it's for the cameras. It couldn't hurt to have pics of them lip-locked.

"How about one more kiss except this time—"

"Bruh, we're done," Chris states it plain.

The photographer hears the severity in Chris' voice and backs away. "A'ight, man. I got it."

Chris rarely shows his assertive side but when he does, folks tend to listen. He only really ever shows it when it comes to Izzie. She wishes he didn't struggle so much with uncertainty. Izzie knows how confident Chris really is, but until he does, she can tell him he's the shit until she's blue in the face and it won't do any good.

"You ready to leave?" he asks.

"Yeah, let's go."

It's the morning of the board meeting. Izzie and Chris are at her place where Chris is making her, what he calls, a power breakfast. He read somewhere that the best type of breakfast before a big meeting is a savory grain bowl. He made her one with roasted tomatoes, sautéed greens, crumbled bacon, and a soft-boiled egg.

"How are you feeling?" he asks, presenting her the bowl.

"Good. I mean, I am a little nervous, but I've been preparing for this since birth. You know how that is."

"Indeed. Grandpa used to quiz me on everything from the best weather for grapes to grow to what sediment was."

Izzie chuckles. "Don't worry, Chris. You and I will both be ruling side-by-side just like we always talked about."

"I hope."

"I know."

"I'm glad you're so confident in me, but we both know I'm not the best at presentations. Remember my oral report sophomore year?"

"That could have happened to anybody. Erections are unpredictable."

Chris looks at her like, "*nice try*."

"I'll tell you what. Since I'm already your girlfriend, I'll be your presentation coach, too."

"Thanks."

"Of course. I'd do anything for you, Chris."

"And I, you."

"Wish me luck?"

"You don't need luck. You're Isobel Brooke Taylor."

"Thanks." She gives him a simpering smile.

An hour later, Izzie steps off the elevator and struts into the Taylor Made office board room. She feels like a warrior going to battle. Self-assured and ready for whatever comes. She picked an outfit especially for the occasion. When she took a selfie and sent it to Heather, she told her that she was giving Miranda Priestly. That's all Izzie needed to hear. *The Devil Wears Prada* is her favorite movie. She's wearing a black pencil skirt that stops at her knees, a black and white checkered tweed jacket with a black leather belt, and stilettos… black of course. Her hair is styled in a slicked-back ponytail without a hair out of place. She had stylists—both wardrobe and hair—over at her house three hours before the meeting to get her look together. Her understated makeup is all business.

Izzie enters the office and is surprised to see the board already assembled. She thought she would get there early enough to get some alone time to meditate—she was wrong.

"Good morning," Izzie smiles.

"Good morning, Isobel," Gordon Petrie, the board president greets her. "Since you're here we should get down to business. Please have a seat."

Why do I feel like I'm in front of a firing squad?

"Isobel, we and the shareholders want what's best for the company," Gordon explains.

"As do I," Izzie replies, confused by his demeanor.

"Look, there's no easy way to say this. Your party girl antics—" Gordon begins.

"I'm sorry, my what?" Izzie says, her voice firm and unwavering.

"What Gordon is trying to say, Izzie, is that Taylor Made needs to continue to be a respectable brand," Sylvia Green, the board vice president says.

"Exactly, and giving a strange man a lap dance at a bar doesn't say respectable." Gordon nods his head, and an assistant turns off the lights as he cues up footage that looks like it was taken on a phone. The footage is of Izzie dancing with a local man during the Taylors' stop in Barbados. His hands are on her hips while she grinds against him. He takes a seat and pulls Izzie into his lap where she keeps up her moves.

"I was just dancing with him. Everyone was dancing like that."

"Everyone isn't up for the job of CEO for a major brand," Gordon argues.

Are they kidding? It's not like I was fucking the guy in public.

"Izzie, there's also the matter of you being seen on a beach in Italy sunbathing topless that floated around about a year ago," Sylvia says. "It keeps recirculating, and it is a growing concern."

Izzie and her parents took a trip to Positano in between their travels to relax before the next leg which included a visit to London and Dublin. A few Black women had set up shop in those two cities with Black hair supply shops to cater to ex-pats now living in Europe. The break was supposed to be relaxing but some guy recognized Izzie and took a picture of her, selling it to TRNN. Turns out the guy was some Black dude from LA on vacation with his girl when he saw Izzie.

How the fuck was I supposed to know someone would recognize me in Italy?

"And we would be remiss if we didn't mention the constant rotation of boyfriends. A lot of whom are celebrities."

I can't believe this. Are they seriously judging my abilities to be an efficient CEO on my private life?

"How exactly is who I date anyone's business?" Izzie's skin heats, and curses she wants to let out, are stuck in her throat.

Gordon rolls his eyes. "Izzie, please don't act so naïve. Dating celebrities has unforeseen risks that can cause harm to you and our brand. We're just grateful that you seemed to have stopped dating questionable men—"

Questionable? He makes it sound like I've dated serial killers.

Gordon continues. "But in the event that your and Christopher Rossmore's relationship ends, it would be wise not to fall back on old habits."

"I'm sorry how I choose to live my life has caused so much concern. That must be terribly stressful for all of you," Izzie mocks.

"Isobel, your flippant attitude and disregard for this board is only going to further you from the role of CEO," Gordon states.

"My flippant attitude is only present because I'm an adult literally being treated as if I'm a rebellious teenager. Let me ask this. Do any of you have any footage of me working? You should have at least seventeen years' worth since I've been working for my father since I was eleven."

These assholes are treating her as if she hadn't gone to every hair show her father attended while he was trying to build the company. Not only did she go, she worked as a hair model right along with her mother. Pretty soon her father had a strong and loyal clientele. Folks were ordering Taylor Made haircare from his website so much that her dad had to hire a full staff to keep up with the orders. After school, once she finished her homework, Izzie would head to her father's office and answer emails from customers. She even worked the phones. Every duty she was assigned led to the past three years. Izzie earned enough of her father's trust to the point when she suggested traveling all over the Caribbean, Europe, and West Africa—building relationships with the salon and hair supply store owners—her father jumped at the idea. But her breasts are what's stopping her from achieving something she earned?

"No one is saying you aren't smart or hard-working, Izzie. We're just concerned about your appearance in the public eye. We need more respectability and less controversy." Gordon replies.

"You all keep using that word like I'm not respectable." Izzie interjects. "And I'm starting to think you all don't have any respect for me or my father. Is that the case?"

"Izzie, please. We don't mean any disrespect to you and especially not your father," Sylvia says, "but you are on the front page of TRNN more than any celebrity. This company doesn't need that type of negative press around it."

"TRNN has nothing to do with the business or how I will run it," Izzie argues. "I am more than qualified to take over for my father. My personal life has no bearing on my abilities. You all know my educational background and the fact that my whole life has been learning all there is to know about Taylor Made. I was literally born into this role."

"I'm sorry, Isobel, but it will take a lot more to persuade us into believing you're ready than your pedigree," Gordan says. "We'll revisit this discussion in six weeks, but, for now, we've decided that your father stay on until we come to a unanimous vote. Or until a suitable replacement has been found."

Each of the board members get up and leave, some giving her apologetic looks. Sylvia and Gordon simply walk past her without giving a second glance.

What the fuck just happened?

5

CHRISTOPHER

Chris pulls up to Izzie's house. It's the twenty-eighth of the month and the first day of the retreat. To put his best foot forward, Chris, the over-thinker he is, wanted to be prepared. He worked on ice breakers for the past two days.

When he called Izzie and asked how the meeting with the board had gone, she was tight-lipped. She said something about it not being a unanimous vote and that she and the board had to meet again in six weeks. That surprised Chris. Why wouldn't the vote be unanimous?

He decided to surprise her with her favorite sweet treat from Carver's Bakery, an apple and cheese Danish with hot chocolate. Chris would like to give her something more intimate that involves them both being naked. These past few weeks with her have been amazing—spending time with her after being separated for so long, and on top of everything else, they've been making out like crazy. So far, it's only been happening when they're out and about, but Chris would like that to change.

There have been more pictures of them on TRNN, so they've got a lot of people fooled. Chris starts to believe he's one of them and constantly has to remind himself that this is just a favor Izzie is doing for him. But, God damnit, if having her in his arms, kissing her, and inhaling her heavenly scent hasn't made him crave more. The thought of him and Izzie being a real couple has passed through his mind before, but he's convinced himself that it wouldn't work because their friendship was too important. He knows Izzie feels the same way because she's been the one to initiate all the relation-ship centered discussions and most of the kissing. The fact that it's only done publicly tells him all he needs to know.

Chris shakes all thoughts of fucking Izzie out of his head and sends her a text informing her that he's here.

CHRISTOPHER

In the driveway. Do you need help
with your bags?

IZZIE

No, thanks. Henri has it.

Henri, Izzie's personal assistant, opens the front door and takes two of Izzie's bags to Chris' car.

Chris notices the look of concern on his face. His brows are pinched, and his eyes are filled with distress.

"Henri, is everything okay?"

"I'll let her tell you." Henri offers.

Izzie comes out wearing a pair of tight black jeans and black stiletto-heeled suede boots. She's wearing a fitted pink t-shirt that says DIVA in calligraphy with her hair pulled back in a bun. Even when looking casual, Izzie manages to look fresh off the runway. The only person who matches Izzie as a fashionista is Heather.

"You look amazing, Iz." Chris smiles at her as she gets in the passenger seat.

Izzie returns a weak smile. "Thanks, Chris."

Chris gets out the car and helps Henri load up the rest of Izzie's bags—seven in total.

After getting back into the car, Chris notices

Izzie staring out the window at nothing. First, there was no upbeat greeting and now she's just staring off into the distance. Normally, she would have hopped into the car and commandeered his phone, picking whatever they're going to listen to during the drive.

"Iz, are you okay?"

"Yeah, I'm good."

"I got you something." Chris offers her the bag housing the danish and the hot chocolate. "I know you can smell what's in the bag."

"No, thank you. I'm not very hungry," she replies.

Okay, what the fuck is going on?

There has to be more to the story than she's telling him, but he decides not to press. When Izzie gets upset—which she obviously is—he knows not to push. She'll tell him when she's ready. Hopefully, she'll be in better spirits when she sees Michaela.

Two hours later, and after listening to several podcasts by Dr. Tariq Brown, they pull up to Hamilton Ranch. Michaela and Hunter hired Dr. Brown to be on site to talk with each couple. Izzie slept most of the ride and is still asleep. Chris stopped to get her a coffee for when she wakes up, so she'll be energized and ready to give her A game. Chris listens to the last bit of Dr. Brown's latest episode. A husband is asking for advice on how to get his wife to stop distancing herself.

"When you say you haven't been the best husband, what does that mean?" Dr. Brown asks.

"Um, I've been unfaithful... a lot."

"Okay. Well, I hate to be the bearer of bad news, but she knows and she's distancing herself so she can get her ducks in a row and leave you."

"Naw, you're wrong. She wouldn't leave me. I'm six foot three, I work out five times a week and I'm good in bed."

"Yeah, but according to you. You two haven't had sex in months, so obviously your sexual prowess isn't that important to her. Also, I can't help but notice that the qualities you chose to point out about yourself are purely physical. What other qualities do you possess that a woman would want?"

"Doc, c'mon, you and I both know that's all women care about. As long as you're a big dude with a beard, getting paid, and always smelling good, they ain't going nowhere. And got I a big dick, too. That's all these bitches care about."

"Then answer me this, sir, why is your wife ignoring you? And why is she included in the 'bitches' you just described. Your wife should get more respect than that."

"Yo, you goin' too far, Doc. I respect the hell out of my wife."

"Then why did you ever cheat on her?"

"Don't have nothing to say now, do you, fool?" Chris mocks the caller.

Men like him really piss Chris off. If there is one thing he doesn't tolerate, it's infidelity. His dad cheated on his mom constantly and with no remorse. She made sure to take his father to the cleaners when they divorced. She enjoys being single and spends most of her time traveling the world, all on his father's dime.

Chris places a hand on Izzie's shoulder before leaning in and softly calling her name a few times.

Izzie stretches and opens her eyes. Her breasts stretch up against her t-shirt. Chris tries to avert his eyes but is having trouble. And now he's back to thinking about her lips and tongue making his dick brick up. They've been friends and only friends for so long and now they're being forced to see each other in a whole different light. It's made Chris again think about if he and Izzie really did try to have something real. He quickly brings himself back down to Earth when he remembers that this is just until he makes CEO, then it's back to being friends. This is no different than any other favor they've done for each other. The difference being that this favor has him wondering about what could be.

"Hi. How long was I asleep for?" Izzie asks.

"Pretty much the whole ride."

"I blame your car. The drive is so smooth."

Her mentioning the car makes him think of Grandpa Sam.

"Thank you," Chris answers, giving her a weak smile.

Izzie cups his face in her hand. "I miss him, too."

This makes Chris feel seen, and this time his smile is warm and genuine. "I know," he gently responds.

Izzie points to the coffee. "Is this for me?"

"Yep."

"Thanks." She takes a sip.

Chris is relieved that she seems to be in better shape than she was when he first got her. He still wants to find out what happened on Monday but he's choosing to wait until she volunteers it.

The luggage rolls heavily out the back as Chris removes it from the car. An attendant appears and looks at all the bags in astonishment. Chris gives him a sheepish smile and a shrug. In need of help, the attendant calls over a buddy and they both get to work taking Izzie's luggage and putting it onto a shuttle waiting nearby. When they have everything on board, the first attendant informs Chris that their things will be waiting for them in their cottage. He then points out the check-in table before letting Chris know that another shuttle will be there shortly to take them to their quarters. Grateful for instruction, Chris thanks him and hands the attendant a hundred dollar bill.

"Showtime," Chris says as they approach the check-in table hand-in-hand.

"Good morning, I'm Erin! Welcome to the Inaugural Hamilton Ranch Couples Retreat. I know who you both are, but we're required to ask for your names."

The Hamiltons were smart picking her to check folks in. She immediately makes you feel welcome.

"No worries. I'm Christopher Rossmore and she's Isobel Taylor," Chris replies smiling warmly.

"Here you are." She hands Chris a key card and a folder. Erin turns to Izzie. "That is such a cute outfit."

"Thank you." Izzie smiles but it doesn't reach her eyes.

Chris takes her hand and squeezes it, causing her to look at him and squeeze back. Whatever is going on with Izzie, they can get through it. They'll figure out a way to achieve their respective dreams and will continue to support each other no matter who or what tries to get in their way.

"Well, surprise, surprise. Fancy meeting you two here."

Chris and Izzie turn around and see his father arm-in-arm with a smirking Trinese.

Oh, come the fuck on!

CHRISTOPHER

After Blake and Trinese check-in, they wait for their shuttle completely ignoring Chris and Izzie.

What the fuck are they doing here?

Great! As if Chris didn't have enough on his plate, now he has to worry about his father and Trinese sabotaging him. He takes a deep breath. When he and Izzie's shuttle arrives, they hop aboard and head to their cottage.

The cottage is gorgeous, they look around admiring the decor—this place deserves nothing less than a five-star rating. Curious of what else the lodge has to offer, Chris reads through the info guide he picked up at check-in. With five thousand square feet, six bedrooms and six bathrooms, this cottage can accommodate up to sixteen overnight guests. And there are six other cottages that look like this, not including the main house. Hamilton Ranch itself is twenty-seven hundred acres with a barn, a gift shop, a museum telling the story of how the Hamilton's acquired the land, and other amenities. Chris can see why so many Hamilton's have gotten married here.

Downstairs there are four bedrooms and upstairs there are two master suites. When Chris opens the closet door, he's taken aback. The space is big enough to host a small soiree.

He comes out and helps Izzie with her luggage. She's frowning at her phone.

"You okay?" Chris asks.

He knows he shouldn't ask her repeatedly, but she looks like she wants to throw her phone.

"Yeah, I'm good. Michaela said something about a welcome breakfast. We should head over to the café and meet them. I can formally introduce you."

"Okay. Sounds good."

Twenty minutes later, they arrive at the café and take a seat at an empty table. Taking all of Izzie's bags into her room took a minute. Chris spots Michaela, and Hunter, laughing and joking with Trinese and Blake.

Fuck me. She's already gotten to them.

A flash of anger surges through Chris. Did they have this planned already? They must have. Chris feels stupid that he didn't see this coming. Parker told Blake about Michaela and Hunter not having their wedding at the ranch. His father and Trinese must have known about this weekend and weaseled their way in. He and Izzie need to nip this in the bud, but when Chris turns to address her, she's still on her phone. Instead of asking her if she's okay for the umpteenth time, he tries a different tactic.

"Do you want to order something?" Chris asks.

"Not really." Izzie still doesn't look up from her phone.

"Do you want to introduce me to Michaela and Hunter when they're done talking?"

"Sure. That works," Izzie replies.

Another couple approaches them and takes a seat. "Hi, I'm Lisette and this is my husband, Eduardo. How are you?" Lisette smiles at Chris.

Izzie finally puts her phone down but only offers a smile. *I guess I'm doing the talking.*

"Hi, I'm Chris and this is Izzie."

"Nice to meet you. So, I'm guessing you know Michaela through your connection to TRNN." Lisette jokes addressing Izzie.

Izzie gives a weak smile. "Yeah. We've known each other for a while."

That's it? C'mon, Iz, you can talk circles around anyone. What's going on with you? Chris awkwardly smiles at the couple.

Michaela and Hunter walk over with another couple, Blake and Trinese.

"Hey, I'm so glad you all were able to make it. Hi, Izzie!"

Michaela comes around the table to hug Izzie who hugs her back and smiles. It still doesn't reach her eyes. Michaela must sense something is off because she turns her attention to Chris.

"Hi, Chris. I don't think we've ever really met." Michaela holds out her hand.

Chris tries to remember the notes he made for making small talk. "We haven't. It's nice to meet you formally."

They shake hands.

"You as well. This is Hunter."

Chris shakes his hand. "A pleasure to meet you."

"You too, man," Hunter says.

"So, how do you like the ranch?" Michaela asks.

"It's beautiful! It reminds me of the episode of *Queens of Artemis* where they go back in time to the old west." Chris answers.

Michaela looks at Chris like he has three heads. The silence is deafening.

Fuck. A snicker comes from Trinese's direction.

"You'll have to excuse my future stepson. He doesn't know how to read a room. Not everyone is a geek, Chris," Trinese jokes.

"I beg to differ," The woman from the second couple says. She turns to Chris. "I love that show! I want them to bring Callie back from the vortex. Oh, sorry. Hi, I'm Jody."

"Hi. And me too!" Chris exclaims.

Oh, thank God! With Izzie being MIA and Trinese being... Trinese, I thought I was fucked.

"Yeah, sorry, Chris, I'm not a big sci-fi person, so I had no clue what you were talking about. Jody and her girlfriend Trish are the biggest nerds on the planet though. You all should get along great," Michaela says.

Everyone laughs.

"Michaela what made you want to host this shindig? I think it's a great idea. Maybe we should do something like it at one of the Rossmore properties," Trinese chimes in.

Chris bites the inside of his cheek. He was too quick to dismiss Trinese. What she lacks in actual skill she makes up for in charisma.

"Well, thank you. It's something that Hunter and I thought up. With the media being awful to me and my family for so long, I found myself becoming distant from my friends, not wanting to go anywhere for fear that TRNN was lurking somewhere. Next thing I know it's been years since I've seen people who I was once really close to. And with Hunter and I getting married soon, I thought who better to catch up with than my friends who are in different stages in their relationships."

"That's beautiful." Trinese turns to Chris. "Tell me, Chris, how long have you been with Izzie? The last I heard you were just friends. When Blake and I met with you the other day, you didn't mention her."

Everyone looks at him.

"I… uh…" Chris stammers.

Please, God, let someone mention sci-fi shit or something. I need another diversion.

"Trinese, don't play the overprotective momma role," Michaela jokes.

"Yeah, you're about the same age as Chris. And he already has a mother," Hunter adds.

"Well, you can't blame me. We are going to be one big happy family soon. Aren't we Chris?" Trinese smiles.

"Yeah, right."

Trinese takes Blake's hand in hers and smiles at him. He responds by kissing her on the forehead.

Of course he's not talking. She's doing all the dirty work. Too bad my partner isn't talking either.

Breakfast is ordered and Chris spends all of it talking to Jody and Trish. Lisette and Eduardo join in the convo too once the subject goes to *Nightshade,* which leads to Jamila Hawkins and her latest project being discussed.

It was a nice time, but Michaela and Hunter still spent the whole time talking to Blake and Trinese. And Izzie's energy was still quiet and off. One thing is for sure, he's going to find out what's going on with her when they get back to the cottage.

7

CHRISTOPHER

Chris didn't want to crowd Izzie, but fuck, between the car ride and the breakfast, he deserves an explanation for her behavior.

He knocks on the door.

"Come in," Izzie answers.

When Chris enters, she's seated on the bed criss-cross apple sauce looking at her phone... again. He lets out a breath. Seeing her on her phone triggers his impatience even more.

"Izzie, we need to talk," Chris says.

"Okay."

She puts down her phone and finally gives Chris her undivided attention. The sternness in his voice surprises him, too. Chris isn't the most confrontational person but when he's lost patience, he can put his foot down.

"Iz, why are we here?"

"So, you can connect with Michaela and Hunter."

"Why?"

"So, you'll be made CEO."

"That's why *I'm* here. Why are you here? You volunteered to be here and be my girlfriend and all you've done is stare at your phone and not talk to anyone. On top of that, every time I ask you if everything is okay, you're vague as hell. Why are you here?"

Izzie's lip quivers and tears form in her eyes. "I…" She starts sobbing.

Oh, shit! I didn't mean to be that harsh.

Chris rushes over to Izzie and holds her in his arms. "I'm sorry, Sunflower. I didn't mean it, I—"

"No, Chris, you're right. I'm so sorry I haven't been there for you at all today, and I've been avoiding you for the past two days. I'm so sorry, Chris."

"It's okay, Izzie."

"No, it's not. I should have been there for you."

"Izzie, calm down." Chris holds her by her shoulders and looks her in the eyes. "What's going on? Talk to me."

"The board…" She sniffles.

Chris runs into the ensuite bathroom and gets her some tissue. She wipes her eyes and calms down.

"The board unanimously voted that my dad stay on until the next vote in six weeks. If they still think I'm a liability to Taylor Made, then they'll bring someone else on."

"How could they possibly think you're a liability?"

"Apparently, my party girl persona and all the coverage from TRNN have left a bad taste in their mouth. They brought up my dating history—"

"But you're supposed to be dating me now."

"Yeah, that's the only thing they agreed was a good thing. They warned me not to fall back on bad habits and start dating actors and athletes again. So, when we're done with our thing, I guess I'll just become celibate."

The idea of their "thing" ending sends a sharp, shooting pain in Chris' chest.

Stop. Izzie's in pain right now. And we're just friends.

Izzie continues. "Gordon Petrie broadcast footage of me dancing with a man in Barbados in front of the whole board room. And they even mentioned the sunbathing pictures."

Those fucking pictures!

Chris wants to find the asshole who shot those photos and choke him out. *If you're on vacation with your girl, why the fuck are you paying attention to another woman's breasts?* And Gordon Petrie is a sexist piece of shit. He always made backhanded comments about Izzie taking over for her father. Whenever Chris would tell her, she eased his mind by saying that the likes of Gordon Petrie didn't scare her.

"What does your dad have to say?"

"He's who I've been on the phone with. Daddy offered to take care of things, but I need to do this myself."

"Iz—"

"Chris, I can't be the daddy's girl who has her father solve her problems. He probably won't be able to do much anyway. He had to answer to the board just like they have to answer to stockholders. That's just how it is."

"Izzie, what I was going to say is *I* can help you."

"How?"

"These assholes only care about money. Their misogynoir bullshit is purely based on the fear that your personal life will affect sales. If they had any common sense, they'd realize you being an It Girl is an asset. So, that's what you should focus on. To them, your ability to dazzle everyone in the room is a problem. You'll show them that not only is it not, but it will in fact bring the company even more money. You've made plenty of contacts over the years with people who have deep pockets. It's time to reach out to some folks. Sound good?"

"Yeah," she smiles and it's real this time.

"I may not know how to schmooze, but I do know money."

"I don't know, Chris. You did pretty well with the other couples. I've always told you that you could conquer small talk and public speaking. You just don't believe it." Izzie pauses then flinches. "Shit, I didn't introduce you to Michaela. I'm sorry."

"It's okay, Sunflower. We have five days to turn things around. So, are you with me?"

"Of course." Izzie hugs him. "And don't think I didn't notice Trinese's ass cozying up with Michaela and Hunter. Don't worry, we're going to beat her at her own game."

Chris hugs her tighter, tickling her rip cage while breathing in her enticing scent of Harmonist Yin Transformation Parfum. Chris notes the orchid and mandarin and unable to help himself, he takes a whiff of her neck.

She giggles and pulls away with a bright smile on

her face. Izzie leans in and gives him a kiss. Chris leans into it.

"Mmmm." She moans as he licks the seams of her lips.

This causes her to slip her tongue in his mouth. As they make out Chris leans in further causing Izzie to lay down on the bed as he climbs on top of her. Chris grabs Izzie's ass and squeezes. Izzie reaches down and massages Chris' dick.

When they kiss in public they try to make it PG —except for that first time at the diner. That was verging on R, but now that they're alone they're heading straight into XXX territory.

Izzie's hand is in Chris' pants. Her soft skin rubs against his dick making him let out a low groan. His hands move to her breasts. Chris slides down her body kissing her neck and chest along the way. He takes a breast out and licks her nipple before taking it into his mouth and swirling his tongue around it. She pulls out his dick and jerks it.

"Uhhh! Chris. Fuck." Izzie moans.

Chris' dick is throbbing in her hand. He's close. Not having sex for over a year will do that. His hands are in her pants, he strums her swollen clit through her panties.

"Mmmmm." Chris is about to explode when—

Izzie breaks away. "Chris, what are we doing?"

"I don't know," He strains to get the words out.

Izzie holds his face in her hands. "Why do I want you so bad?"

"I don't know, but I want you even more."

"We should… oh my God…" Izzie steadies her breathing. "We should get some air."

"That's a good idea. Give me a minute though. I'll meet you at the door."

"Okay."

Chris gets up and adjusts his clothes. He walks carefully to his room. His dick is as hard as steel. He enters his ensuite bathroom, takes his dick out, grabs some lotion and gets to work.

Twenty minutes later, Chris and Izzie are walking around the ranch when they stumble upon the barn.

"Let's go check it out." Izzie takes his hand before he can protest.

As they walk closer Chris can hear the horses' neighing sounds grow nearer. "You know what? Why don't we go check out the museum instead?" Chris suggests.

"Why? We already know who the Hamiltons are," Izzie says, as she continues to walk toward the barn.

Neeeiiggghh! One of the horses lets out a loud neigh.

"Ah, shit!" Chris jumps.

Izzie giggles. "Chris, don't tell me you're still scared of horses?"

"Fine, I won't tell you."

Chris looks around like he expects a horse to pop up behind them.

Izzie laughs. "Come on, you need to get this monkey off your back."

"Hell, I would prefer monkeys, they're less unpredictable than horses."

"How?" Izzie looks at him like he's insane.

"You expect monkeys to start flinging shit everywhere. You don't expect a horse to fling you off it's back."

Izzie silences her phone and Chris' so as to not startle the animals. Gently, she grabs his hand and walks Chris into the stables, immediately approaching one of the horses.

"Izzie, don't. They're murderous beasts." Izzie smirks at him as she goes to a nearby storage unit and retrieves an apple. She feeds a horse named Sparkle the red fruit.

"Hi, sweetie. Tell Chris you're not a murderous beast."

"Lies." Chris looks at all five horses with his eyes squinted in suspicion.

"Chris, that incident with the horse happened when you were ten."

"It threw me into a pile of hay! I'm lucky I didn't break something."

"So, you've said." Izzie cups Chris' face and giggles.

"Stop it with the sexy giggling. It's not funny. Besides, need I remind you that a horse paralyzed—"

"Oh, God. Chris, please don't bring up—"

"Superman. Superman, Izzie."

"Christopher Reeve." Izzie finishes her statement in defeat. She clears her throat and puts her hands on Chris' shoulders. "Christopher Reeve has been resting peacefully for years now and even after his accident he led a fulfilling life continuing to act and doing philanthropy."

"I know that."

"Then, sweetie, you really need to let this go."

"Never!" Chris declares. He points at each horse. "Fuck you. And fuck you and fuck you. And definitely you. You look evil."

The last horse Chris points to is all white with reddish looking eyes. Hell, even Izzie has to admit that thing looks like a demon.

The demon horse neighs loudly causing Chris to jump into a kung fu pose.

"What are you doing? You don't know any martial arts," Izzie says.

"Shh! It doesn't know that."

"Why are you shushing me? It's a horse. It can't understand us."

"Fine. Whatever. Can we please go now?"

Izzie rolls her eyes. "*Fine*. You big weirdo. It's time for us to rejoin the others anyway."

They make their way over to one of the many gardens on the property. This one is called the Kimber Garden. Just like the cottages, each garden is named after one of Parker Hamilton's kids. Someone who didn't know much about the family would think this was a sweet gesture by a father. The gardens are actually named after the children he disinherited as a "fuck you." In comparison, Parker Hamilton makes Blake Rossmore look as loving as Philip Banks.

As Chris and Izzie enter the garden, they see Hunter talking with Blake.

Trinese is standing near Michaela who seemingly looks frazzled by the food options at the lunch bar.

"Chris!" Jody calls.

He and Izzie make their way across the room to

join Jody, Trish, Lisette, and Eduardo at a close by table where they're enjoying various beverages and chatting.

"Hey," Chris greets them.

"Hi, I'm Izzie. Sorry for not being talkative earlier. TRNN was being a thorn in my side, as usual," Izzie smiles.

"Totally understandable. No need to apologize," Lisette replies.

"If it makes you feel better the comments section has been on your side. Especially defending Chris," Trish adds.

Chris and Izzie look at each other and at the same time check their phones. The headline is ridiculous and makes them both laugh.

Chris Rossmore: Farmer's Market Hero!

Our photog was only trying to get a quick snap of Ms. Izzie Taylor when Chris Rossmore lost it, screaming "stay away from my woman!" We have witness accounts of the incident.

"I did not say that. And what witnesses?" Chris chuckles. He leans over and whispers to Izzie catching a whiff of that incredible scent. He swallows and speaks softly. "These people are really the reason the board won't vote unanimously?"

"I know right?" Izzie turns to look at him.

Their close proximity causes them to stare at each other longingly. They rub noses and breathe in each other. Chris wants to take Izzie back to their cottage, take off all her clothes and—

"Hey, lovebirds. You realize we can see you, right?" Jody laughs.

Chris and Izzie chuckle at their faux pas.

"Are you fucking kidding me?" Michaela yells into her phone.

Everyone looks at her. She mouths, "I'm sorry," before walking a few feet away with Hunter and Trinese on her tail.

"Is Michaela okay?" Chris asks.

"You would think having a rich daddy would afford one the ability to throw a wedding in three months' time, but Michaela is running into some problems," Lisette answers.

"Yeah, apparently a lot of folks are getting married in May as well. They all reserved most of the things Michaela wanted and it's left her scrambling," Jody asserts.

Michaela paces back and forth while Hunter holds her hand and Trinese talks her down.

"No offense to your future stepmom, Chris, but she needs to fall back. We've known Michaela for years. When she gets like this it's best to give her space. I'm sure Izzie knows," Trish watches them.

"It's true," Izzie agrees.

"She's been in Michaela's face this whole time. Someone should warn her," Eduardo remarks.

"She'll figure it out." Chris shrugs.

He takes another look and sure enough, Michaela looks like she's about to go off. Blake seems to be able to read the room and places a hand on Trinese's shoulder urging her to back off. They make their way to the table and join the others.

"Hi, all." Trinese smiles like she wasn't just tap dancing on someone's nerves a few seconds ago.

"Hey," Most of the table replies.

Trinese looks over at Chris and Izzie. "So, you two never told us how this thing happened between you."

Isobel

Chris looks at Izzie and smiles. She winks at him with an impish grin that says, "watch me work."

"Chris and I started seeing each other four months ago when I was still overseas. His grandfather had passed two months before and while I couldn't be there for him in person, I made sure to contact him every day after it happened." That's not a lie. Izzie called Chris no matter the time each day after Grandpa Sam's passing.

Izzie continues to speak.

"Even being separated by thousands of miles didn't deter anything. I realized after years of being friends I wanted to be there for him in every way. It's sad that it took a tragedy for us to finally see each other, but I think Grandpa Sam would be happy."

She looks deeply into Chris' eyes while caressing his face with the back of her hand then scratching this beard. Her fingers make their way to his lips where she traces them with her fingertip, causing him to kiss each finger.

"He would," Chris says cupping Izzie's face in his hand.

"That is so romantic," Jody says, placing her hand over her heart.

"Oh, here she goes," Trish says. "You two just had to get her going."

"Hush, Trish. You big ole grump," Jody says. Everyone laughs but Trinese and Blake.

"How long have you and Trish been together?" Chris asks.

"We've been together for three years. We moved in together after a month. We're basically a big walking lesbian stereotype," Jody answers.

"That's right! Jody here even drives a Subaru." Trish jokes. Everyone laughs but Trinese and Blake again.

"Why did you decide to come to the retreat?" Izzie asks.

"To get away from her mom," Jody says.

"Babe, don't start."

Jody rolls her hazel eyes. "Trish's dad passed away a few months ago too."

"I'm so sorry to hear that," Chris says.

"Thanks," Trish says. "Anyway, my mom moved in, and it's been an adjustment for JoJo."

"That's because she keeps trying to steamroll over every decision we make. Trish is used to it and just lets her have her way, I'm not as flexible. We just needed a few days away from her."

"I'm sorry. Having an inflexible, bullheaded parent isn't easy," Chris replies making Izzie giggle.

Good one, Tiger.

Blake is about to reply when Izzie cuts him off. "What about you two?" She points to Lisette and Eduardo.

"We've been together for nineteen years. We met in high school."

"Us too!" Izzie cheers.

"Yeah, but unlike you two, we started seeing each other not long after we met. We have four kids that range in age from two to fourteen and we needed a break," Lisette says.

"A much needed one. Dealing with the terrible teens and the terrible twos at the same time has been a lot," Eduardo says.

"Did you all see that the ranch has a spa?" Izzie asks. "You two should definitely take advantage of it."

"Oh, yeah. We most definitely are hitting that up." Lisette replies.

"Hi, all. Sorry we've been having some wedding issues." Hunter says, pulling out a chair for Michaela to sit.

"Yeah, but we're glad to see you all getting along and chatting," Michaela says.

"Michaela, remember if you need any help, let me know." Trinese smiles at her.

"So, you've said," Michaela replies flatly.

Knowing this is going to be tricky, Chris and Izzie exchange glances. It is clear the wedding is obviously getting away from Michaela—a notorious control freak— so mentioning booking Rossmore is a risk.

A shuttle arrives to take everyone on a tour of the ranch. The moment they near the barn, and a horse neighs, Chris becomes jumpy again. Izzie takes his hand and squeezes it, and he kisses the back of hers in return. Later the group has lunch together. Lunch became a group hangout which included dinner.

By nine that night, the shuttle begins its route to drop everyone off at their cottage. When it's Chris and Izzie's turn, they waste no time rising to their feet.

"Don't forget game night tomorrow, you two," Hunter shouts before Izzie and Chris get off the shuttle.

"That's right. We're going to have some fun and base the questions on things each individual loves. It's a fun way to see how much their significant other knows about them. Chris, your subject is fashion," Michaela adds.

"That works." Chris smiles.

"And Izzie your questions will pertain to—"

Michaela checks her phone. "Ah, here it is. *Lord of the Rings*. See you at breakfast tomorrow."

The shuttle drives off with the others waving at them; they wave back with smiles on full display.

Izzie looks at Chris with trepidation. She managed to get into comic books—much to her surprise—but she couldn't get into *Lord of the Rings* no matter how much she tried. She just couldn't get past why they couldn't just use the damn eagles to get to Mount Doom. When Michaela asked her guests to fill out a questionnaire about their partners, Izzie answered the question *"What piece of pop culture does your partner love?"* with *Lord of the Rings*, not thinking anything of it. She also listed various comic books, too. Why the hell couldn't Michaela have chosen that? Or *Game of Thrones?* She would have killed at that.

Reading her mind, Chris touches Izzie's shoulder. "It's okay, Iz. We'll bow out of game night. We'll just hang out while everyone else plays."

"Chris—"

"It's okay. By the way, your story of how we got together was incredible."

"I'm sorry. I know bringing up Grandpa Sam must have been a sore spot."

"No worries. He passed recently, so not bringing

him up wouldn't have made sense. Besides he always used to tease us about when we're going to get married, remember?"

"Yeah." Izzie smiles at the memory. The last time she spoke to Grandpa Sam he told her, *"My son doesn't have the sense God gave a chicken, which is why he can't keep a woman. But Chris does. Ya'll need to make this happen."* Izzie giggles at the memory.

Chris kisses her on her forehead. "Good night, Sunflower."

"Good night, Tiger."

Chris heads to his room when he looks back at Izzie, he flashes a smile. She smiles right back before he closes the door, then she heads to her room.

Izzie pulls out her laptop and sits on the bed. "Time to get to work."

8

ISOBEL

Cocktails and game night has been a ball. Refresher drinks in hand, Chris takes a seat and offers Izzie a Cosmo while he has a Manhattan.

The day was awesome as well, filled with laughter and jokes between everyone except, of course, Blake and Trinese. Blake has spent most of his time on his phone while Trinese has been tucked under Michaela. At one point, Hunter had to pull Michaela away from the group. Jody joked that they should all take bets on how long before Michaela goes off on her.

"Okay let's keep things going. Chris, can you name Izzie's favorite fashion centered film?" Trish asks.

The object of the game is to guess your partners

favorite things pertaining to pop culture but with a *Newlywed Game* twist. One partner is asked a question and after they answer, the other partner will turn over a card with the correct answer to show the other participants if they're significant other had the correct response.

"I can do you one better," Chris replies "I can name five of them in order of her preference. First and foremost is *The Devil Wears Prada*, followed by *Confessions of a Shopaholic, Mahoghany,* and the last two are TV shows. *Sex and the City* and *Ugly Betty*."

"Izzie?" Trish asks.

Izzie flips her card over and sure enough she has all five listed on her card. She gives Chris a kiss on the cheek.

"Good job, Rossmore," Lisette cheers.

"Thank you." Chris playfully bows making folks laugh.

He's killing it! That's my Tiger.

"Okay, Izzie—"

"You know what, I'm going to be answering questions for us. Izzie doesn't need to." Chris interjects.

"No, Chris, it's fine." Izzie smiles at him.

"Sunflower, you don't have to do this. I know how much you hate *Lord of the Rings*."

"It's fine, Tiger," Izzie purrs.

Chris relents and nods at Trish signaling for her to keep going.

"Okay, Izzie, what is Chris' favorite part of the Two Towers?"

"That's easy, the Battle of Helm's Deep. Specifically, the part where Gandalf leads the Rohirrim cavalry."

Chris looks at her with wide eyes like she just explained how to successfully perform brain surgery. That's understandable. When Chris told her about how much he loved the trilogy, her eyes involuntarily glazed over. Up until last night, Izzie couldn't name a single character. She once called Gandalf 'Dumblepuff.' She's not a fan of Harry Potter either.

"Chris?" Trish asks.

Chris is so busy staring at Izzie that he doesn't hear Trish.

"Chris!" Lisette calls.

"Huh, what?" Chris turns to the others.

"Did Izzie get the answer right?" Trish asks.

Chris turns the card and yep! Izzie got the answer right.

"Yes!" Izzie claps.

"Okay, let's give the lovebirds five points each.

Next question, Izzie, this is for you again. What's Chris' favorite scene from *Return of the King*?"

Izzie turns looking Chris in the eyes and replies, "Chris' favorite scene is the one where Sam asks Frodo if he has any memories of the Shire. Frodo tells him no and that he can only see the ring and the eye, so Sam carries him the rest of the way. Chris would always say that the devotion Sam showed Frodo reminded him of us. He told me that whenever I needed him to, he would always be there to carry me. No matter what."

Izzie looks around at the group and sees Lisette and Jody tearing up.

"There you two go getting Jody all mushy again." Trish teases. "And Izzie is absolutely correct. That is Chris' favorite scene. Five more points for you kids."

It's midnight when Izzie and Chris enter the cottage.

"I can't believe it! You... you... Izzie, how did you?"

"I stayed up all night yesterday boning up on all things LOTR. I remembered you mentioning the parts you enjoyed. I had the context based on what you've told me. After that, all it took was looking it up and memorizing all the parts you love."

Chris stares at her in wonder. "You did that for me?"

"I'd do anything for you, Chris."

Chris pulls her into his arms. "I never thought a scene between Sam and Frodo would make my dick hard, but here we are."

Izzie laughs rubbing the back of her hand against Chris' face. Chris turns his head and kisses her fingers. This is quickly becoming one of her favorite things.

She knows this isn't right, but she can't help herself. The way Chris looked at her when she gave the correct answers and the way he's looking at her now… she wants him. Bad. So fucking bad.

"You never told me, Iz. What's your favorite sexual position?"

"I like most of them. I don't have a specific favorite, but I do like being told what to do, and I enjoy being punished if I don't obey."

"You like BDSM."

"I love soft BDSM."

Chris wipes his mouth. "Sorry, my mouth started to water."

Izzie giggles.

"Isobel?"

"Yes, Christopher," she answers, her face inches from his.

"May I eat your pussy?" He rubs his nose against hers.

Izzie nods her head vigorously. "Dear God, yes!"

Chris picks her up and carries her to his room. He places her on the bed and lifts her skirt, pulling her panties to the side before partaking of his feast.

"Oh, my God! Chriiiiiiiss." Izzie pushes the back of his head deeper between her legs.

Chris licks and nibbles her folds causing her to squirm. He slides his tongue inside of her twisting it around—French kissing her pussy.

"Oh, fuck! Chris, let me sit on your face," Izzie cries.

"Go ahead."

Chris lays on his back and Izzie pulls off her panties and straddles his head. He grips her ass and continues devouring her. Unable to control herself, Izzie thrust her hips forward riding his face. He moans as he slurps up Izzie's wetness.

Hearing him moan makes her wetter. "Shit! Ah, feels so fucking good. Do I taste good, Tiger?"

"Fuck, yes! Your pussy is sweet as hell."

Izzie is close to coming. Her head feels light as

she claws her nails down the wall while Chris flicks his tongue along her clit. Tears stream down her face. She's so close. When Chris sucks her clit into his mouth, she loses it and gushes all over his face.

"Ah! Chriiiiisss!" She screams.

Izzie's eyes grow heavy, she falls over and passes out on the bed.

When she wakes up and looks at her phone, it's five in the morning. She turns and sees Chris asleep beside her.

What the fuck did we do? This changes everything. We can't go back to just being friends. Fuck! What was I thinking? Chris... Mm! He was just so sexy and irresistible.

Izzie gets out of bed and goes to her room. She finds a pair of sweats and a pair of low-heeled shoes and changes. Inside the nightstand she finds stationery and writes Chris a note.

Went out to think, I'll be right back.

Izzie returns to his room and leaves the note on his nightstand before heading out the door and walking to the barn.

She walks past the sheep when her phone rings. Loudly. She forgot to put it on silent near the animals. The ranch hands dealing with the barn animals and the one in the stables handle their respective animals swiftly, but the one dealing with the sheep—who he just let out—can't control them. And now they're running. Toward Izzie.

Shit!

9

CHRISTOPHER

Went out to think, I'll be right back.

Chris reads Izzie's note again. *Shit!* He came on too strong. Her pussy was heaven on his tongue, but he can't help but to feel some regret. They're best friends, and he may have fucked up everything between them for a few moments of pleasure. Now she's wandering the ranch probably wondering how to break it to him that they can't be intimate anymore. He tried calling her, but she didn't answer. Knowing Izzie, she's probably back at the barn. Chris grabs his neatly folded clothes from a drawer and changes. He needs to make sure he didn't fuck up things between them. As he grabs the doorknob, his phone rings. It's Izzie.

Oh, thank God!

"Chris! They're chasing me."

"Who is?" Chris yells angrily.

Whoever is fucking with Izzie is about to get their ass beat.

"The sheep!"

Wait, did she just say sheep?

"Sheep are running after you?!" Before Izzie can answer, Chris jets out the door and runs straight to the barn. A few horses nearby let out neighs, causing Chris to damn near jump out his skin. He sees the sheep going after Izzie in the distance, and a ranch hand trying to gather them.

"Aaaahhhhh! Stop it!" Izzie screams. She runs to a nearby tree and fruitlessly tries to climb it.

Chris looks around for a shuttle or a golf cart to rescue Izzie and comes up empty. He turns his attention to the stables.

You're going to need a horse. You can do this! Do it for Izzie. Chris hightails it to the stables and goes straight to Sparkle.

He's grateful and a tad bit disappointed that there's no ranch hand to stop him from the dumb ass idea he's cooked up.

"Hey, there. You remember me? I called you all murderous beasts and flipped you off. I'm here to say I'm sorry and I didn't mean it," he says calmly. "And I need your help."

Chris opens the pen and Sparkle slowly walks out. Carefully, Chris places a saddle on her back and tries to hop on, but before he can secure himself onto her back, Sparkle takes off.

Chris screams, "Oh, shit! I'm gonna die!" Quickly, Chris manages to get himself onto Sparkles back. *Thank you, core strength. I gotta pay my trainer more money.*

"Aaahhh!" Izzie screams as one of the sheep takes one of her shoes.

"Izzie," Chris breathes. Unyielding, Chris pulls the reins with his right hand closer to his chest, hoping it'll direct the horse toward Izzie.

"Go to the nice lady who gave you an apple." And she listens! Sparkle turns and trots toward Izzie.

"Chris!" She calls out.

"Izzie, don't worry I'll save you," Chris yells. Sparkle runs past Izzie. "No, go back!"

Sparkle doesn't listen and instead dumps Chris into a large inflatable pool clearly being used as a watering hole for the cows. Drenched in water and specks of wet hay, Chris stands and rings out some of the water.

"Why is there always fucking hay? And I take

back my apology," Chris calls out to Sparkle as he climbs out of the pool.

The cows—who don't spook as easy as the sheep—just stare at him.

"Hello, cows," Chris says. He scours the fields until his eyes land on Izzie. He then runs to her, shooing away the sheep. "Move, get away from her!"

A ranch hand and a couple of border collies are already near Izzie and manage to redirect some of the sheep. Another one hands Izzie back her shoe before handling Sparkle. She lets out another snort directed at Chris.

"Yeah, fuck you too," he mutters. Chris reaches the tree Izzie managed to climb. She's seated on a long, thick branch. "C'mon, jump down. I'll catch you." She jumps off the branch and into his arms. "You okay, Sunflower?"

"You rode on a horse."

"I rode on a horse… kind of."

"You rode on a horse for me." Izzie has tears in her eyes.

"I rode on a horse for you." Chris smiles. "I'd do anything for you."

The two lean in and are about to kiss when Chris feels the adrenaline wearing off and gets light-headed.

"Oh, God. I got to sit down." Chris stumbles onto the ground and takes a seat. Izzie wraps her arms around him and rest his head on her shoulder.

———

THE CREW LAUGH THEIR ASSES OFF. CHRIS AND IZZIE are talking to them via FaceTime.

"You actually got on a horse!" Heather cackles.

"Yes." Chris rolls his eyes. "And it promptly threw my Black ass in a watering hole."

He has since changed his clothes having given his soiled sweats to an attendant to be washed. The attendant chuckled when they came to pick up his laundry. Apparently, what happened to him and Izzie is the talk of the ranch.

"The money I would have paid to see that," Artie laughs.

"Fuck you, Art." Chris readjusts himself. He's currently sitting on a donut with an ice pack between his legs. His ass is sore, and his genitals hurt.

"Leave him alone. Chris is my hero." Izzie argues.

She kisses him on the cheek making his face flush.

"Aw!" the crew all says at the same time.

"Shut up." Chris chuckles.

"Something more happened. Ya'll are holding out on us," Freddie assesses.

Chris and Izzie look at each other like two kids who got caught dipping into the cookie jar.

"I knew it!" Freddie cheers. "Did ya'll finally fuck?"

"Not exactly, and what do you mean finally?" Chris asks.

"You know what, Heather has been waiting thirteen years to say this, so we'll let her have the floor. Go ahead, Heather," Artie says.

"Gladly. You two are idiots," Heather announces.

"What the hell?" Chris scowls.

"Screw you, Heather," Izzie frowns.

"Listen. Both of you. Do not talk, just listen. You two have been in love with each other since high school but you both convinced yourselves otherwise. Izzie, answer me this. Why did you ask Chris to sit with us back in the day?"

"Because kids were teasing him, and he was so sweet and didn't deserve it."

"So, it had nothing to do with Pamela Charles?"

"The senior?" Izzie asks.

"Yeah, Izzie. The senior. Sure, Chris was teased. Hell, people talked shit about me and you. Teenagers are petty as hell, but you make it seem like we rescued Chris. He was just so adorably clueless that he didn't know that there were girls at our school who liked him. Pamela Charles being one of them. And you asked Chris to sit with us *after* you found out she liked him. She may have been a senior while we were only sophomores, but you were more popular than her. You used your popularity to get to Chris before she could."

"I don't remember it that way," Izzie replies.

"Of course you don't." Heather rolls her eyes and continues. "You two goofballs have been so busy convincing yourselves that you're not in love that neither of you realize me, Art, and Fred have been here watching you two fumble any chances of actually getting together for years now."

"How did we fumble anything?" Chris asks.

Heather shakes her head. "Simple. Chris, you thought you could never bag Izzie, so you never tried. And, Izzie, Chris thought you were his friend out of pity, so you never tried to bag him thinking he wouldn't take you seriously. Meanwhile, you two would bad mouth each other's boyfriends and girlfriends to the three of us. And every time y'all were around each other y'all looked like you were about to fuck in front of everyone."

Chris thinks about the comment Jody made about everyone being able to see them. He was literally thinking about fucking Izzie at that exact moment.

Maybe there is something to what Heather is saying.

"And most importantly, have you two ever noticed how you both talk about each other?" Heather asserts.

"How do you mean?" Izzie asks.

"Chris, describe Izzie," Heather orders.

"Izzie is a baddie. She's smart, gorgeous, kind, and funny. She lights up any room she's in. She's ethereal."

"Now Izzie, describe Chris," Heather says.

"Chris is brilliant, sweet, funny, charming, handsome, and dreamy." Izzie shrugs.

"Seriously, are you fools listening to yourselves? Ethereal? Dreamy? Who the fuck describes their friends that way?" Heather says exasperated. "You two morons are in love with each other, and you always have been."

Chris takes in Heather's words and realizes she's right. He is in love with Izzie. She must be thinking the same thing because she looks just as stunned as him.

"Now back to my original point, what happened between you two?" Freddie asks.

"I ate Izzie's pussy," Chris confesses.

"And before that, Chris played with my clit while I jerked him off and he sucked on one of my tits," Izzie admits.

"But ya'll are just friends," Heather smirks. She turns her attention to something going on behind her. "Alright, ya'll I have to go. My little cousins just woke up and I can't have them hearing what we're talking about."

Heather exits the chat.

"I have to head out too. I've got rehearsal in an hour," Freddie says.

Freddie dips.

"I'll talk to you kids later. You two definitely have a lot to talk about," Artie remarks.

Artie ends the chat.

Chris and Izzie look at each other and reply in unison. "Yeah."

10

ISOBEL

Izzie and Chris sit on the sofa in the living room. She hands him a bottle of water then opens hers and takes a sip.

"I could have gotten that," Chris insists.

"I'm pretty sure your dick and balls are broken. And your ass is still sore."

"Touché." Chris looks at her with a curious grin, like he's seeing her for the first time. "So, you liked me in high school?"

"Yeah," Izzie replies, her face flushed.

"So, what you're telling me is that my Urkel looking ass had a shot with you?" Chris asks.

"Yes. I mean, it's not that unrealistic. Steve pulled Myra and eventually Laura."

"Yeah, but you typically dated, and still date, gym rats."

"You are a gym rat, sweetie."

"I wasn't back then."

"I know, but you were so sweet. And then we became friends and…"

"And?" Chris asks.

"Chris you actually liked me. Not Isobel Taylor, bad bitch. You liked Izzie who would talk your ear off about clothes and who made you watch every episode of *The Wow Factor*.

"I still think Chrisette and Gabby should have won season three," Chris says.

The Wow Factor is a reality show where an aspiring designer teams up with an aspiring fashion model. The winners, respectively, get a contract with a top agency and a job at a top fashion house. Not exactly Chris' cup of tea. But he watched a marathon with Izzie when she was sick; in addition to making her soup. He always does stuff like that. He's always there for her.

She continues. "My point is while other guys were busy trying to have sex with me, you were happy with just being in my presence. You didn't try to take advantage of me."

"I would never do that."

"I know you wouldn't."

"If I'm being real, Izzie. I honestly thought you approaching me that day was a prank."

"Seriously?"

"I didn't know you that well. You were the pretty, popular girl in some of my classes. You seemed nice, but I was leery. Part of me kept that guard up. I guess I thought all these years that if I admitted my feelings, I'd risk losing you."

"You could never lose me, Chris." A smile brushes across Chris's lips. "Chris, are you…? Do you…?" Izzie starts.

"Yes, Izzie. I love you. I'm in love with you. Always have been. Heather was right. We are idiots." He laughs at the last part.

She joins in his laughter before becoming earnest. "I love you too. I love you so much."

Izzie scoots closer to him and kisses him. Chris takes her face in his hands and kisses her back. She climbs into his lap and straddles him. His hands move to her ass, hers to the back of his head. Chris suddenly breaks the kiss.

"Chris?"

"Ow. Sorry, I think my dick and balls still need time to heal. But I still love you." Chris' brows knit and he grits his teeth. He's clearly in pain.

Izzie immediately hops off his lap. "I'm sorry, Tiger."

"It's okay, Sunflower."

Izzie shakes her head. "Tiger and Sunflower. We really are idiots." They laugh.

Izzie and Chris arrive for breakfast an hour later hand-in-hand.

"Hey you two!" Michaela greets them. "Oh, my God! Are you both okay?"

"Yeah, we're good," Izzie answers. *Better than good.*

"So, your phone went off and scared the sheep?" Hunter asks.

"Yeah, that's on me. I didn't silence my phone when I was by the animals, and it spooked the sheep. I'm so sorry, Michaela," Izzie explains.

"It's okay. The animals tend to wander away sometimes. Thankfully, this is a large ranch, so they can't wander off the property. If you spot any sheep just call the front office. There's somebody there twenty-four-seven," Michaela adds.

"How many wandered off?" Chris asks.

"About three out of twenty of them. Don't worry, they'll get found. I'm just glad you're both okay."

"Chris, one of the ranch hands said you hopped on a horse," Lisette chimes in.

"You're scared of horses," Blake says. He doesn't

say it like he's surprised. More like he's stating a fact to embarrass Chris. Trinese chuckles.

Assholes.

"Wow, look who's not all up Michaela's ass and who actually managed to look up from his phone to say something. You two realize you're supposed to be participating like the rest of us, don't you? You haven't joined in anything we've done over the past three days. Quick, what are their names?" Chris points to Lisette and Eduardo.

Blake and Trinese don't respond. He simply fiddles with his phone while she looks speechless.

"Okay, how about these two?" Chris points to Trish and Jody.

Chris notices Michaela and Hunter looking at them, waiting for an answer. They still don't respond.

"Interesting, it's almost as if you two are here for something other than the retreat," Chris asserts.

"What about you, Chris? Why are you here?" Trinese asks.

Chris turns and points at Izzie with a smile. "I'm here because of her. I'm here because she suggested that we come, and I'm glad we did. Being here helped us discover that our love isn't something that we found recently. It's always been here. Ever since day one. It just took us a few years to recognize that. Now that we have, we're never going to forget it. I love you, Izzie."

"I love you too, Chris."

Chris takes Izzie by the waist and pulls her to him then kisses her senseless. When they break apart, Izzie swoons and falls into Chris' arms. He looks down at her and laughs. She feels giddy and warm. Her skin prickles as she giggles like a teenage girl. If she were an emoji or a cartoon, she'd have heart eyes.

"Michaela, Chris and I are going to have to skip breakfast. We'll see y'all later," Izzie says still staring at Chris.

Chris picks her up and carries her back to their cottage. Their new friends, laughing, and whooping behind them.

11

ISOBEL

Chris takes Izzie into her room and sits her down on the bed.

"Are you okay to do this, Chris? I'm coming down from the high you gave me with that kiss, so maybe we should chill for a bit."

"I'm fine. Besides if I don't fuck you soon, I think I might die," Chris replies.

Izzie laughs. "That's awfully dramatic."

"It's the truth." Chris runs his fingers through her hair as he gazes at her. "Guess what?"

"What?"

"I read up on being a soft dom."

"You did? When?"

"After my shower, but before we called the crew."

"Chris, that was like two hours ago. You can't learn about being a dom in two hours."

"No, I know, but I think I could give it a try." Chris gives her a piercing glare. It's both sexy and intimidating. "Tell me what you need from me Izzie."

"I need to be your one and only."

"You already are."

"I need you to cater to my every desire."

"Done."

"I need you to keep me in line when I disobey."

"That'll be fun." He gives her a wolfish grin.

"And finally, I want to be spoiled beyond belief."

"Pffftt." Chris gives a dismissive wave of his hand. "That's light work for me, Sunflower."

"Good to know. I love the confidence by the way." Izzie simpers.

"Glad you approve. And now that you know that I'm standing on business." Izzie giggles. Chris continues, "I need you to stand up and take off your clothes for me."

Izzie stands from the bed and removes her capri pants and button-down blouse. Next, she removes her bra and then her panties. His eyes roam her body from bottom to top. When he reaches her eyes, he approaches her and gets on his knees. Chris traces his tongue along her belly. He takes her nipple into his mouth before circling his tongue around her areola. His hands run up the back of her legs and land on her ass where he digs his fingers into her flesh. Izzie's head falls back. He manages to straddle the line between pleasure and pain perfectly. Chris takes a gentle bite of her nipple then moves to her other nipple licking, sucking, and biting.

"Do you like this, Sunflower?"

"Yes," Izzie whispers.

"Good. Lay down and spread your legs."

Izzie lays down on the bed and opens her legs. Chris gets on his belly in the sniper position and slowly licks Izzie's pussy. She throbs and clutches the bed sheets. He slips his index finger inside her.

"Your pussy is so pretty, Izzie."

"Thank you."

Chris softly kisses her pubic area. It's hairless except for a sliver of hair down the middle. Chris kisses her there before licking and kissing the waxed areas again.

"Oh, that feels so good."

Chris sucks on her folds before separating them and fucking her with his tongue.

Izzie closes her eyes. The only sounds in the

room are her moans accompanied by his moans and slurps. It's a symphony of ecstasy that makes her move her hips like she and Chris are slow dancing. Every move is choreographed by their passion. Izzie opens her eyes when she no longer feels Chris' tongue.

"I need you to come back down to Earth, Iz." She looks at him and he smiles. "Are you back with me?"

"Yes."

"Good."

Chris climbs out of the bed and proceeds to remove his shirt. He playfully flexes making Izzie giggle. She sits up on her knees and watches. He unbuttons his jeans and slowly unzips them. The anticipation and torture make her want to get out the bed and *help*.

"You stay right where you are." Chris orders.

"How did you--?"

"I know you, Sunflower. Plus, you had the mischievous gleam in your eye."

Izzie laughs. "You're right."

"I know I am. You just be patient. I have to go slow, remember?"

"Right, I was so scared for you when I saw you on Sparkle's back."

"Shiiiitt, I was scared too." He laughs.

Chris pulls down his pants carefully followed by his boxers.

Yowza!

Chris dick is… wow. Feeling it was amazing, especially when he started throbbing in her hand but seeing it is everything.

"Can I suck it, Chris?"

"Later."

Chris gets back into bed and lies on top of her. He leans down and peppers kisses all over her shoulder and neck. She runs her hands up and down his back as his dick brushes against her pussy.

"Chris," Izzie pleads. "I need you."

"You have me. I'm right here. You're mine and I'm going to take good care of you. Okay?"

"Okay," She grins.

"Do you have protection?" Chris asks.

"I do but I want to feel you. I had physicals once a year when I was away, and I didn't sleep with anyone in the last two years. I'm good. You?"

"I'm good too. The last time I had sex was 2022, and I was tested not long after."

With all the details out the way, the two go back into their passion-filled bubble where Chris kisses

Izzie as intensely as he did around the others. Their tongues mingle and do a dance of their own. Both of their mouths filled with the sweet flavor that is her. Izzie is grateful she's already lying down when he breaks the kiss and gives her pecks on her lips. Chris lines his dick up with her wet opening and pushes himself inside her.

Izzie's breath is caught in her throat as she adjusts to his size. He grunts as he slides deeper inside of her.

"Chrisss," She hisses.

"Iz," Chris lets out a strained whisper. "Oh, shit."

"You okay?" Izzie breathes.

"I'm good. You're just so tight and wet. And you're throbbing. I..." Chris takes some breaths. "I gotta be real with you, I'm not exactly sure how long I'm gonna last."

"That's okay." Izzie tongues him down.

"Mmmm." Chris groans.

She breaks the kiss. "As long as I have you, that's all that matters."

"God, I love you," Chris chokes out.

"I love you too."

Chris gives her slow thrusts. "Goddamnit, Izzie. You feel incredible."

"So do you, Tiger. Ohhhh." Izzie shakes at the heavenly sensation surging through her body.

"So, fucking beautiful." He kisses her. "And sexy." He kisses her again. "You're mine. You're all mine. Tell me, Izzie. Tell me you're all mine."

"I'm all yours," she cries.

Chris keeps going as Izzie wraps her legs around him. She can feel wetness slide down her ass.

Chris starts to move a little faster and Izzie matches his rhythm.

"Fuck, Izzie. I'm so close."

"Me too."

"Do you have a toy?" Chris asks.

"Yeah. I have a vibrator in my bag."

Chris chuckles. "Which bag? You brought seven remember?"

"It's in the small pink bag in the corner." Izzie points.

Chris slowly pulls out causing Izzie to clench.

"Goddamn, Iz." Chris grits his teeth.

"Sorry."

Chris gets out the bed and turns Izzie on her side smacking her ass.

Izzie yelps then giggles.

Chris finds the vibrator and swiftly gets back on top of Izzie. He places the vibrator on Izzie's clit and turns it on… at least he thinks he does but it's not doing anything. Chris hits it a couple of times.

"Tiger, it's not a remote. Whacking it is not going to work." Izzie laughs.

"Well, then how the fuck do you turn it on?" Chris turns it around over and over.

Izzie takes it out his hand and twists the bottom, actually turning it on before handing it back to him.

"Whatever happened to vibrators where you just press a button?" Chris grumbles.

Izzie laughs some more but those laughs quickly turn to moans when Chris places the vibrator back on her clit. He slides his dick back inside her and pumps in and out of her with vigor.

"Oh, fuck, Chris. Uhhhh!" Izzie catches up matching his rhythm again.

Chris chuckles. "You're not laughing now are you, Sunflower?"

"No." Izzie purrs.

"Good."

Izzie and Chris continue to move in syncopation. Chris raises the level of the vibrator.

"Uhhhh!" Izzie moans. "Chrisss! Oh, fuck."

She shuts her eyes. The sensations coursing through her throbbing pussy are non-stop. Her breath is short and her mind is blank.

"Izzie, look at me. I want to look into your eyes as you come."

"I can't it's too much."

"Open your eyes, my love," Chris whispers in a voice that denotes sternness and patience. "Do it, Izzie."

Izzie opens her eyes and they immediately well up with tears. Chris' face is so handsome. His intense and loving expression makes her senses explode. Soon, Izzie has tears streaming down her face. She comes. It's like nothing she has ever felt.

Chris takes her face in his hand, lifting her chin when she briefly looks away.

"No. Keep your eyes on me. Don't look away, Izzie."

Izzie cries, "I love you, Chris."

"I love you more." Chris comes. "Fuck, Izzie."

His voice barely audible.

The two stare at each other, Chris wipes Izzie's tears and, having formed some of his own, she does the same.

"I'm going to take care of you now, okay, Iz?" Chris asks.

Izzie smiles and nods her head, surprised she can even manage the action of moving any part of her body. She feels like she's seeing Chris for the first time. The earnestness in his face almost makes her cry again. His expression reads just how willing and able he is at taking care of his Sunflower. His brows are slightly pinched, and his eyes are dark and bewitching. Izzie's senses are on high alert. Seeing Chris, feeling his soft skin and toned body makes her never want to stop touching him. Smelling his aroma of sweat mingled with Terre d'Hermès is overwhelming her. It's all overwhelming her. He must realize how she's feeling because Chris smiles back, gathers her in his arms and kisses her.

"C'mon, I'll carry you." He offers.

"That works." She replies.

IZZIE LAYS ON THE COUCH WITH HER FEET IN CHRIS' lap. His warm hands fully grip her arches as he massages. While she's enjoying her foot rub, Izzie indulges in some sushi Chris ordered for lunch from a local Japanese eatery. For a moment, they ramble about how much fun this trip has been and Chris tells Izzie about a cute little town not far from the ranch with shops, cafes and boutiques. Excited, Izzie squeals and makes Chris promise to take her before they leave.

"Did you really bad mouth my exes?" Izzie asks.

"You have dated some meatheads." Chris presses his thumbs into the arch of her foot.

"Oh my God! I can't tell you how good that feels," Izzie groans.

"It's those high ass heels you're always wearing."

"You leave my Loubous out of this." Izzie playfully frowns.

"Don't get smart with me, Izzie. Not unless you want to get spanked," Chris says in a tone that says he's dead serious.

Izzie decides to be a brat. "You wouldn't dare."

Chris pulls her by her legs onto his lap and flips her over. He smacks her ass repeatedly then rubs it.

"That too much?" he asks.

"No."

He continues to spank her making her squirm and moan. Lifting her off his lap, he gets on his knees and licks her ass cheeks. He pulls her panties off and licks, kisses, and bites her ass before running his tongue down her ass crack. He flicks his tongue across her pussy. It feels so good and she's so wet. He flicks her clit, moving his tongue rapidly. She's so close. It's building.

Yes! Oh, God, it's coming.

Then he stops, sits his Black ass back on the

couch, turns her over, and goes back to rubbing her feet.

"What the fuck, Chris?!"

"You were being bratty." He looks at her. "You didn't think that would go unpunished, did you, Sunflower?" Chris winks at her.

"You're mean," Izzie whines.

"No, I'm not." Chris picks up her foot and kisses it. "I'll make you come later. Finish your sushi." Izzie takes a bite of her sashimi and pouts.

"Stop pouting or I'll make you wait longer," Chris warns.

Izzie fixes her face. *Man, he learned a lot in those two hours.* Izzie remembers what they were discussing before she foolishly talked herself out of an orgasm.

"So, you thought my boyfriends were meatheads?"

"A few of them. Darren was definitely a meathead. He kept challenging me to arm wrestle him."

"Yeah, he was pretty threatened by you. I guess he had a reason to be."

Chris chuckles. "Yeah, but even he wasn't as bad as Hazel."

Izzie rolls her eyes. "That girl was annoying, but

then again you always seemed to date prissy, controlling women like her."

"I did not"—Chris begins. He must have thought better than to argue 'cause he stops and stares at Izzie, who is giggling—"Shut up." He teases.

That makes Izzie burst out laughing which earns her tickles to her feet making her laugh even harder.

12

CHRISTOPHER

After spending all day in the cottage with Izzie, it was time to rejoin the rest of civilization.

The event this evening is a pajama party movie night. Izzie wears a cotton number with cartoon candy and Chris has on a t-shirt and sweatpants. He wraps his arm around Izzie's waist as they enter the ranch's screening room, and claim two seats in the back.

"I'll get us some popcorn," Chris says.

"And gummi bears, please," Izzie smiles sweetly.

"Of course. What would you like to drink?"

"You know what I like."

"Damn right I do, now what do you want to drink?"

Izzie laughs. "I'll have a Sprite."

"Coming right up." Chris heads to the lobby and takes his place in line.

"Hey, Chris," Eduardo says.

"Hey."

"Came back to join the land of the living I see," Jody teases.

"Yeah, Izzie and I—"

"Please, we don't need to hear the dirty details," Lisette jokes.

Chris chuckles. "You sure? It's pretty dirty."

"I'm listening," Eduardo replies.

"No, you aren't. You don't need any ideas. We have enough kids," Lisette argues, and they all laugh.

Chris notices Michaela is standing in a corner with a distressed expression. *Is she okay?* His instinct is to approach her and ask what's wrong, but she looks like she's about to explode.

Of course, here comes Ms. Can't Read the Room and her companion Sir Slithers A Lot making their way into the theater. Immediately, Trinese leaves Blake's side to run over to Michaela. Chris can't hear what Trinese is saying but Michaela's voice becomes loud. Very loud.

"Jesus Christ, will you leave me alone! Allow me to enlighten you. We are not friends. The only reason why you're here is because my dad asked me to invite you two."

I knew it!

Michaela continues her rant. "All you've done this whole time is get in my face, try to chat me up about Rossmore Wines and get me to hang out with you. Back off!"

Jody turns around and makes eye contact with Chris then mouths the words, "I called it." No, shit she called it, anyone would the way Trinese had been all up Michaela's butt since arrival. Chris raises an eyebrow, sticks his hands in his pockets and looks ahead at the menu making Jody chuckle. This is good, but he can't let Blake know how happy he is about it.

Trinese walks away holding her head up like she didn't just get put in her place. Chris can feel her eyes on him. She's no doubt giving him a dirty look, there's no point of giving her the satisfaction of attention so he doesn't even bother looking at her. Blake joins her and whispers something in her ear as they walk into the screening room.

The others head into the screening room with their treats.

Chris hears crying. He turns and sees Michaela wipe her eyes. *Okay, I can't ignore that. Hopefully she doesn't yell at me.* Chris makes his way over to Michaela. "Are you okay?" he asks. When she raises her head, she's frowning causing Chris to hold his hands up in surrender. "I'm just checking to see if you're okay. I swear. I won't even mention my last name." Chris jokes.

That makes her chuckle. "I'm fine."

"Are you sure?"

"Yeah."

"Okay." Before Chris can leave to return to the concession stand Michaela begins to talk.

"It's just that nothing about this wedding is going right. I just want to be married to the man I love and have a beautiful ceremony to celebrate it. The only thing that's come together is the wedding venue."

Well, I guess that's the end of that. Though the news is disappointing, and Chris knows his chance at CEO is still in jeopardy, he's more concerned about Michaela. Wanting to spend the rest of your life with the person you love and celebrating that with friends and family shouldn't be so stressful. Rossmore has hosted its fair share of weddings and seeing dozens if not hundreds of "happy couples" become bundles of anxiety on their special day made Chris consider eloping. However, now that he and Izzie are the real thing, he knows that's absolutely out of the question.

He'll just have to mitigate any stress Izzie might have by taking on most of the load when their time comes. Which begs the question…

"How's Hunter dealing with all of this?" Chris asks.

"He's more concerned about me."

"Where is he tonight?"

"He had a meeting with the director of the next film he's composing. He couldn't get out of it."

If Michaela's family is media royalty, Hunter's is film royalty. Although he's good looking enough to be an actor, Hunter decided to become a musician, composer, and conductor. He's scored countless movies including films directed by Claude Laurent and starring Ann Marie Laurent his parents—who are legends. Their immense fame is the reason Hunter goes by Lawrence instead of his real last name.

"Well, I know we don't know each other that well, but if you need any help, I can contact some folks. I know quite a few vendors; I've built strong relationships over the years and a few of them owe me favors."

"Thanks, Chris. I have to admit, you and Izzie confused me. You seem so introverted and she's definitely not." They both chuckle because she's not wrong. "But I'm glad she hit me up. You two are so sweet together and you seem like a real cool guy."

"Why thank you."

They exchange smiles as Chris gives Michaela an one arm hug. He's happy she feels better.

Izzie comes out to the lobby. "Say Rossmore! Where's my popcorn, Sprite, and gummi bears?"

"You want to wait even longer for your treat?"

"I've already been waiting—" Izzie pauses realizing what he meant. "No, sir."

"Okay then."

"You two need a moment alone?" Michaela asks.

"No, we're good," Chris says.

Michaela heads to the screening room but turns around and says, "Thanks again, Chris."

"No problem."

Curious, Izzie tilts her head and side-eyes Chris. "What was that about?" she asks.

"I'll tell you later." Chris wraps his arms around Izzie and guides her to the concession stand.

When they return to the screening room, everyone fixes their attention on them.

"Michaela has informed us that because you two kids won the trivia game you get to pick the movie. So, what are we watching?" Lisette asks.

Chris turns to Izzie. "You pick, Sunflower."

"So, what'll it be, Izzie?" Jody asks. "*The Devil Wears Prada, Confessions of a Shopaholic* or *Mahoghany?*"

"*Avengers: End Game.* Chris and I both like that movie."

Michaela pulls out her phone. "I'll inform the projectionist."

Once they take their seats, Chris and Izzie snuggle up and get cozy, Chris kisses her forehead gently. This is all he could ever want.

13

ISOBEL

Saturday was a free day, so Izzie and Chris spent the day in town near the sushi restaurant he ordered from earlier in the week. The small town was so enchanting that Izzie sent an email to her realtor about getting some property there. It was then that she saw a text from Artie. He works in PR, so he tends to know stuff regarding the press before any of them.

ARTIE

Izzie, the people are on your side.
Big time! Take a look at TRNN's
latest article and the comments.

Izzie opens the link and places her phone in the

middle of her and Chris so he can read along with her.

Where are Izzie and Chris?! The Couple Dujour is laying low. Trouble in Paradise, already?! Tell us your thoughts.

"Leave them folks alone. They're probably afraid to leave their house the way ya'll keep bothering them."

The truth is Chris and Izzie, along with the other retreat guests, signed a waiver stating they wouldn't divulge what happens this weekend. No one is allowed to take pictures, that includes staff. That's the only reason TRNN doesn't know about the sheep chasing/Sparkle incident.

Izzie reads more comments, and to her surprise, they're all standing up for her and Chris.

"They aren't bothering anyone. Why are you niggas at TRNN so pressed about them?"
"If I were him, I'd have her in my bed all goddamn day. You'd never see our asses."

They both laughed at that one since that's basically what they did on Friday. Seeing so many people on their side made Izzie's heart soar. *Let's see the board argue with this.*

Between trying to get the public's approval and all the wheeling and dealing Izzie has been doing before she meets with the board, she's feeling much better about her chances next month. A few of the ideas she's working on include a make-up line and Taylor Made brand of bust downs that will no doubt make them millions.

They also talked about some of Chris' options since Michaela and Hunter have a venue. Turns out they're getting married at the Musée Rodin. Compliments of Jody, who relayed this valuable information. It's where they had their first date. Izzie could tell Chris was disappointed even though he tried to hide it. Obviously, he was concerned that Michaela and Hunter kept running into roadblocks but getting them to agree to have their nuptials at one of the wineries would have been amazing. Rather than sulking in what could've been, Izzie and Chris spent Saturday night coming up with ideas on how to still get him the job of CEO.

"How's this? I could pitch the idea of their engagement party or rehearsal dinner at Rossmore.

They could have it a week before they head to France," Chris says.

"I like that," Izzie replies. "And you could offer them a deal, like having them post the pics on IG and tagging Rossmore Wineries. I think if she can control the narrative, Michaela may be up for sharing stuff on social media."

"Couldn't hurt to ask." Chris agrees.

LATER THAT EVENING IZZIE AND CHRIS ATTEND THE retreat farewell party. Tomorrow they will meet with Dr. Brown before hitting the road to head home. Thank God Blake and Trinese left earlier that day, something about an emergency at one of the vineyards. *Bullshit.* Chris hasn't heard from Paula the whole time they've been here, so what emergency could there be?

Michaela and Hunter have spared no expense on the farewell party. They hired a DJ, a top-notch caterer, and the décor is immaculate. The interior is made to look like Play's house from *House Party.*

Chris and Izzie sit on the couch chatting and kissing. "You want to dance?" Chris asks before licking and sucking on Izzie's neck.

"Mmmhmm." She nods and moans.

"Good. I'll request a special song for us."

"Okay."

Chris goes to the DJ and whispers something. Seconds later "Big Ole Freak" by Megan Thee Stallion comes on.

Izzie looks at Chris like, *"you're joking right?"*

He approaches her. "I haven't seen you twerk in a minute."

"Silly Tiger." Izzie playfully rolls her eyes.

"C'mon. Please." Chris begs. Even getting on his knees. He smiles up at her. "You know you want to. There's no TRNN, and nobody's going to take a picture. Even if they did, everybody loves us as a couple so who cares." Chris gets up and offers his hand. She scrunches up her nose but smiles while taking it.

When Izzie and Chris hit the dance floor, Izzie immediately dips it low and makes her ass shake. Chris gets behind her, pulling her up so her ass is directly on his dick. She winds her hips in circular motion on his crotch.

"This might not have been my best idea," Chris admits.

"I know, I can feel you poking me. Want to get out of here and poke me for real?" Izzie smolders.

"Fuck yes." Chris goes to grab their coats but before they head out, Michaela stops them.

"Wait you two!" Michaela catches up to them, Hunter jogging right beside her.

"Don't worry, we weren't going to leave without saying goodbye." Chris assures her.

"I would hope not," Michaela chuckles.

"We wanted to thank you for coming to the retreat," Hunter says.

"Yes, having you here has been great. However, we do have an ulterior motive for stopping you. We won't keep you. You both clearly look like you want to get out of here. But Chris, you mentioned knowing some vendors the other day."

"Yeah, who do you need me to contact?"

"We need a vendor for wine. Not just for the wedding but the events leading up to it. The bachelorette party, engagement dinner, and the rehearsal dinner as well," Hunter replies.

"Do you know anybody?" Michaela smirks.

"I may be able to help with that, yes."

"Perfect! We'll all have to meet up for lunch soon."

"Sounds good."

"Good night you two," Hunter says.

"Good night. We'll make sure to say goodbye before we head out tomorrow," Chris assures.

The happy couple wave goodbye and head back to the party. Chris and Izzie walk back to their cottage. When Chris opens the door, he lifts Izzie in the air.

"Hell yes! That's what I'm talking about." He cheers twirling Izzie.

She laughs uproariously. "You did it, Tiger!" she cheers.

"I did! I really did!"

"I knew you could."

Chris puts Izzie down, but she still keeps cheering and jumping up and down. She notices where his eyes are.

"You really like my titties."

"I *love* your titties," Chris corrects her.

Izzie undoes her red corset top and takes it off throwing it at Chris' feet. She grabs her breasts and squeezes them before lifting one to her mouth and licking her nipple.

Chris' eyes look like they're about to pop out his head. "Do that again." Izzie does what she's told, except she takes both breasts and licks her nipples. Chris closes his eyes and groans. When he opens them, his expression has changed from tortuous pleasure to stern boss. His brows are still furrowed but his posture has straightened noticeably more.

"Please come here and get on your knees," he requests.

Izzie walks to him and sinks to the carpet, leaving her eye level with his crotch. Chris takes off his belt and undoes his jeans. She pulls out his stiff penis and kisses it before taking his dick in her mouth.

"I didn't tell you to do that, yet," Chris smirks.

Izzie takes Chris dick out of her mouth and places her hands on her lap. He cups Izzie's face in his hands, making her look up at him.

"I love how eager you are to please me," Chris teases.

"Very eager," Izzie agrees.

Chris takes his dick and rubs the tip against Izzie's plump lips. She wants to kiss it so bad, but she waits. She knows she'll be rewarded for her patience.

A full five minutes pass, and Izzie remains on her knees waiting for Chris' instructions.

"You're being nice and calm. Good job, Sunflower. You're doing very well."

"Thank you."

"You are more than welcome. Go ahead and open your mouth." Chris says quietly but with a rough edge.

Good God! This man could convince me to buy Crypto.

Izzie opens her mouth and Chris slides his dick in. Closing her lips around his throbbing member feels unbelievable. Her tongue traces over his veins enjoying the feel of his thickness. Clearly, he's enjoying it.

"Shit," Chris harshly whispers.

"Mmmmm." Izzie moans.

Izzie pulls away and yanks Chris' pants and boxers to his ankles. After moving closer, she takes Chris back into her mouth and sucks his dick like her life depends on it.

Chris holds both sides of her head for balance. Izzie can see his knees buckling but he remains standing. She decides to send him over the edge— sure it may get her spanked and punished, but making Chris lose it will be worth it.

She deep throats his dick, sucking it deeper into her mouth and gagging on him.

"Ohhhooo!" Chris eases himself onto the ground.

Izzie lets his dick out of her mouth and sees the

fruits of her labor in the form of Chris' come. She takes the head back into her mouth and coaxes him to come again. It works. Chris shoots another load, this time into Izzie's mouth. She sucks it all up before pulling away and swallowing. She opens her mouth to show Chris she swallowed.

Izzie stands and removes her pants made of red lace. Next goes her panties, also red lace. She approaches Chris, who is now lying flat on his back with his eyes closed. She uses her spit as lube and jerks his dick back to life. His eyes flutter as he gets harder.

"What happened?" Chris says.

"You kind of passed out."

"I did what?"

"It's happened before you'll be fine."

"No wonder your exes would always beg for you to take them back," Chris says.

"Yep," Izzie smiles.

Now standing over Chris, she slowly squats down until her pussy brushes up against the tip. She sinks down onto his dick causing Chris to clutch her ass. Izzie starts bouncing on his dick before sinking herself deeper.

"Ahh," She whimpers. "You're so big, Chris."

"You're so tight," He chokes out.

Izzie pushes her hips forward and Chris matches her thrust for thrust. Izzie leans down as she pushes her hands down into Chris' chest.

"Oh, shit." Izzie's eyes roll to the back of her head.

Chris holds on to her ass for dear life. She's definitely going to have some finger-sized bruises after they're done. Knowing she's going to have Chris' mark on her does something to Izzie. She thrust her hips forward faster, and Chris tries to keep up. Once they have a rhythm, they both moan loudly unable to form words. He's throbbing inside her. She knows he's about to explode.

"Sheep!" Chris screams as he fills her up.

Wait, did he say sheep?

Izzie takes Chris' face into her hands. "Chris, are you okay? Are you having a stroke?"

Breathless, Chris mumbles, "Behind you."

Izzie turns around and sure enough there are two sheep standing outside the sliding glass doors of their cottage watching them.

"Go away. We're doing grown folks' things. And don't think for a second that I forgot about my shoe." Izzie gestures a shooing motion with her hands which does nothing. Both sheep bah in response. "We should call the front office."

"Yeah, we'll do that once I can feel my legs," Chris says as he falls asleep.

"Chris?" Izzie leans down so they're face to face. Chris softly snores making Izzie giggle. The sheep bah again. "I don't think that's going to wake him, but thanks anyway."

14

CHRISTOPHER

Chris had to get two coffees this morning. One large and one medium to make sure he didn't fall asleep during their appointment with Dr. Brown. Honestly, Chris just wanted to meet him. Getting his insights on Chris and Izzie's new relationship is a plus.

"It's nice to meet you both," Dr. Brown says.

"You as well," Chris says.

"It is my understanding that you two have been best friends for thirteen years, and have recently realized your true feelings for each other. What has that felt like?"

"Amazing. It's like we're still Chris and Izzie, but we have this whole other part of our relationship that has gone undiscovered," Chris explains. "It's weird but if feels like we're meeting each other for the first time while simultaneously knowing everything about each other."

"Yeah, a lot of my clients who were friends first before becoming lovers said something similar. I have to ask a very personal question. Has sex entered the equation yet?" Dr. Brown asks curiously.

"Yes, quite a few times," Izzie says, her eyes downcast and her face flushing.

How does she make being adorable so fucking sexy?

"While I want you to enjoy this new aspect of your relationship, I do want you to be aware that sex can become a crutch when couples find they no longer have anything to hang onto, even a couple who were friends first. I think the two of you should try not having sex just for a week and see how this new phase fares without the physical to fall back on."

At the same time, they rebut.

"Hell no." Izzie states it plain.

"Yeah, that's not happening." Chris asserts.

"It's not forever you two, just for a week."

"Izzie?" Chris asks.

"Nope," she replies without giving it a moment's thought.

"You heard the lady," Chris tells Dr. Brown.

Dr. Brown laughs. "Okay well in that case just

remember to be honest with each other and while acknowledging the friendship you two share don't forget to focus on your love story that is really just beginning."

"Thank you," Izzie says sweetly.

"Yes, thank you so much, Dr. Brown. It was great to meet you; I listened to all of your first season on the way here."

"Thank you. Always nice to meet an admirer. Best of luck you two."

"Thank you," they both reply. As Chris and Izzie head back to their cottage to get ready for the road trip home, Chris' phone buzzes. It's a text from Blake.

BLAKE

Be in the office at nine sharp tomorrow morning. Me, you, and Trinese are having a meeting.

Chris shows Izzie.

"This is it," she says.

"I know. Neither of us booked it, but at least I have something to present. Either way I passed his test."

"You damn sure did."

It's nine sharp as Chris waits outside his father's office. Fifteen minutes later, Blake and Trinese show up walking arm and arm giggling.

"Good morning, Christopher. Please come in," Blake greets.

Chris enters and just like when Blake issued the challenge, he sits across from Blake who is seated at his desk and Trinese standing beside him. Again, Chris feels like a kid in the principal's office. All the progress he made getting out of his comfort zone only to be placed back in it with a glance from his dad.

"Chris, I have decided to make Trinese the new CEO."

"Wait, what? But she didn't secure the Hamilton-Lawrence wedding."

"Neither did you."

"That may be, but if you check accounts receivable, we just got a huge payment from Hamilton Media. I secured wine for every event Michaela and Hunter will be having leading up to the wedding and for the wedding itself. I should be made CEO."

"Well, it doesn't matter because I was never going to make you CEO anyway."

Chris must be hearing things. *Did this mother-fucker just say what I think he just said?* "Why?" Chris asks.

"Because I never wanted you. You were your grandfather's son and never mine. That man left you everything. You!" Blake barks making even Trinese jump. He continues. "You. A sniveling little shit who can't put two words together without fumbling. You, who would go whining to him or your money hungry mother every time 'Daddy wasn't nice to you.'"

There's a moment of silence, Blake appears as though he's trying to calm himself. His chest rises high and falls putting Chris on edge. "I was twenty-eight when you were born, and my father determined that I needed to be more responsible, so I was forced to marry your mother and raise you. And I have resented every second of your presence. I honestly thought that after I got sick, he and I could get past our differences, but he still doted on you. It wasn't until he got sick that he handed over the keys and I'm not letting them go."

This can't be happening.

"But no worries, Christopher, you can take over when I'm dead cause that's the only way you'll get ahold of this company. As of now, I would sooner burn all of this to the ground than hand over the reins over to you."

Chris can feel tears stinging his eyes and his throat feels like there's a lump of coal stuck there, making it hard for him to talk. He needs to keep his mouth closed anyway. The bile has risen and no doubt he'll throw up if he tries to speak. With his pride at the forefront Chris swallows his feelings. Eventually, Chris finds his voice and tries not to make it quiver. "Then why promote Trinese if you're still going to be in charge?"

"Because I can. Now every time you get an email from the CEO, you'll see her signature and know it's not you," Blake sneers.

"What makes you think I'm going to stay here?"

"Because you will." Blake smirks. "Where else are you going to go? You know this place inside and out. It's in your blood. It's all you've ever known. You owe too much to your grandfather to leave. So, you won't."

Chris sinks in his chair. He's right. Chris wouldn't leave. He'll fight. He'll fight for his rightful place at Rossmore Wineries. He'll go against his father, and he'll win. He just doesn't know how yet. As long as Blake is in charge, there isn't anything he can do. His grandfather made Blake the CEO and never changed leadership. Afterall, why would he? At that point, Blake had them both fooled.

Chris let out a breath and locks eyes with his father. "Are we done here?"

"We are. I believe your talents are needed back in private events. Please close the door on your way out."

ISOBEL

IZZIE HAS BEEN TRYING TO REACH CHRIS ALL DAY. She's been busy with wig manufacturers and labs specializing in make up for melanated skin, so when she had a moment to call during her breaks, she finds it peculiar that she hasn't gotten a response yet.

Later that night, hoping he's had enough time to get his bearings, she decides to go to his condo. They've been besties since forever so of course she has a key and lets herself in.

When she enters, Izzie hears "Killing in the Name" by Rage Against the Machine. She follows it to Chris' home gym where he's hitting a punching bag, no doubt picturing his father.

The hair on the back of her neck stands on end as

she watches him hit the bag over and over, harder and harder.

I'm going to kill Blake. Izzie goes to the sound system and turns the music off causing Chris to whirl and face her. He looks like he's ready to strike whoever turned off the music, until he sees Izzie.

"Please turn that back on."

"No, Chris. We need to talk."

"I don't feel like talking, Izzie." Izzie approaches Chris with a rag and wipes the sweat from his brow.

"Tell me everything that happened."

Chris takes off his glasses then takes the rag from Izzie and wipes his face. "Let me take a shower first."

"Do you want me to join you?" Izzie asks.

"No, thank you."

Oh, shit. He's definitely upset.

An hour later, Chris comes downstairs from his room dressed in basketball shorts and a T-shirt. Izzie has a supreme pizza ready and a bowl of kettle corn with the *Lord of the Rings* trilogy cued up. To top it off there are two frosty mugs of root beer floats on the coffee table. He smiles but even with him smiling Izzie can't help but notice that the sparkle in his eyes has dimmed.

She takes a seat on the couch and pats her lap for him to lay down. He rests his head on her lap as she starts the *Fellowship of the Ring*. Izzie keeps the volume low enough for him to talk when he's ready to.

"My father hates me," Chris finally says.

They're at the part in the movie where the hobbits meet Aragorn. Izzie mutes the movie and rakes her manicured nails across Chris' scalp. Chris sinks his head deeper into her lap and tells her everything. When he's done Izzie remains verbally silent, her distaste for Blake growing by the second. *I'm sure Artie has to know some shady people who can kill Blake and make it look like an accident.*

"Izzie," Chris says.

"Hmm," She answers her thoughts being disrupted.

"You can't kill my dad. I finally have you and I'm not giving you up for a prison sentence. I'll have to bust you out and then we'll be on the run."

Izzie belts out a laugh. "True. What do you need me to do?"

"You being here is enough."

"Then here you have me," Izzie says and proceeds to continue raking her nails over his head plotting what they should do next.

CHRISTOPHER

Chris, Izzie, Michaela, and Hunter are having lunch at a café. For the past three weeks, Chris has been working from home. He knows it makes him look weak, like he can't face Blake or Trinese, but he doesn't care.

Walking the halls of the Rossmore Wineries main office used to fill him with pride. Seeing his last name on the building—knowing one day it would all be his—had been a lifelong dream. If he can't make it come true, he doesn't know what he'll do.

"Thanks again for the wine hook up, Chris," Michaela says. "We're scheduled to have a tasting in a few weeks at the Malibu location."

"Happy to help."

Chris flashes his best fake smile. It seems to

appease Michaela and Hunter, but Izzie is not so easily fooled. She doesn't miss a beat. Last night she told him she knows he's hurting, and to her credit, she's done everything in her power to help make him feel better.

"I swear I don't know what I'm going to do. It seems like everyone and their mother decided to get married in May," Michaela says, "and now Ms. Chantel Stone has run off with my hair stylist and make-up artist. Apparently, she's going on tour, and hand-picked them to be on her glam squad. I heard she's paying beaucoup bucks for them to go on the road with her for a year."

"I can help you with that," Izzie suggests.

"Yeah, Iz is in the process of making a deal with some Black women in STEM to create a makeup brand for Taylor Made, and they've already gotten her some samples," Chris brags.

"That's right, and I know tons of hair stylists thanks to working alongside my father for so many years. I can put you in touch with the one we met recently in Barbados. She's amazing! She'll need to be flown out here but here's some of her work." Izzie hands Michaela her phone showing her the stylist's website.

Michaela instantly gasps. "This is beautiful! I love

it, and I'd love to meet with the women who are working in the lab!"

"That can be arranged," Izzie says, smirking like she knows she just won Michaela over.

"Thanks, Izzie, and if this all works out, I'd happily make sure that Taylor Made is prominently shown during the filming of the events and the ceremony."

"That would be fantastic, Michaela. Thank you."

By the end of the lunch date, they had Michaela and Hunter in the bag. The couple agreed to have the weeks leading up to their wedding be filmed, and to air it on Hamilton Media's streaming service as a reality mini-series in the fall. Michaela mentioned that she's tired of hiding and wants to use their nuptials to create her own narrative without the likes of TRNN interfering.

Chris is proud of Izzie. Folks focus so much on her looks that they forget how brilliant she is. Her business acumen should be studied. She's making all the right decisions that will lead to Gordon Petrie and the rest of the board eating crow. *Maybe I could get a job at Taylor Made.* Thanks to Izzie, Chris knows all there is to know about fashion and haircare. It'd be one of the smoothest transitions.

"No sweat. Anything to help a Black woman break that glass ceiling. I swear I don't know how you ambitious types do it. If Daddy left me everything, putting me in charge of Hamilton Media, I'd want to pull my hair out," Michaela says.

Chris and Izzie make eye contact, and she winks at him. This could be because she knows that the news of Trinese's promotion hasn't been released yet. Blake isn't planning on announcing it until he "steps down" in June. That gives Chris three months to figure out what to do to get them away from what his grandfather built.

THAT NIGHT, IZZIE LAY BEFORE CHRIS NAKED AND blindfolded while he ties her wrists together.

"That too tight?" he asks.

"No, not at all."

"Good," he says, "how do you feel, Sunflower?"

"Eager."

"Good. Keep those legs open for me, okay?" Chris has been thinking so much of what his next move will be career wise that he needed a break. When he told Izzie he needed a distraction, she suggested a little bondage. He's been studying more BDSM and has wanted to show her his knot tying skills. Now's as good a time as any.

"Okay." Izzie agrees.

He pulls out a vibrator from his bag of tricks by the bed and turns it on. "You hear that?" he asks.

"Yes," She smiles.

"And it's a simple push button. Not that weird twisty shit you had." Chris teases.

"Duly noted, Tiger."

Chris turns on the vibrator and pushes it to the second level before he places it on Izzie's clit.

"Oh!" Izzie squirms.

Chris takes the vibrator off her clit. Izzie hips immediately thrust up missing the sensation. "Did I ever tell you how pretty your pussy is?" Chris asks before taking a lick.

"Only every time you see it."

"It warrants repeating. You are stunningly beautiful, Izzie. All of you." He kisses down her inner thigh to her knee.

"Thank you," She simpers.

"Did I ever tell you what I thought when I first saw you?"

"Was it something about my boobs?"

"That was the second thing I thought. The first was whoever is with her must be more worthy than Thor."

Izzie giggles. "I should have known there would be a comic, fantasy or sci-fic reference."

"Of course you should've. You're slipping, Sunflower." Chris turns the vibrator back on pushing it to level three before placing it back on her clit.

"Oooo! Chris. Oh, my God." Chris moves the vibrator around in a circular motion. "Mmmm. That feels so good." Izzie whimpers. He takes the vibrator off causing Izzie to whine. "Nooo!" she says, thrusting her hips again. Chris wraps his lips around her folds, sucking and licking while holding her up by her ass. He's eating her out like she's a juicy ripe melon.

"Mmmm." Chris enjoys the taste of her on his tongue and the feel of her wetness around his mouth. "You know you got me addicted to your taste, right?"

"You got me addicted to you tasting me."

"You're so fucking sexy, Izzie."

"So, are you."

"You ready for me to fuck you?"

"Yes."

"Tell me. Tell me how bad you want me to fuck you," Chris orders as he lifts her up and carefully turns her on her stomach.

"I want you to fuck me so badly. More than I want Taylor Made."

Damn. I don't think a woman has ever wanted me to fuck them that badly. Chris rubs her ass cheeks then bites each one. "I'm not one to ever leave you hanging."

"No, you aren't, and that's why I love you."

"I love you too."

Chris pushes his dick inside her slippery opening and pounds into her like he's trying to get her pregnant. Izzie throws her ass back so hard and fast her cheeks shake like a bowl of Jello.

"Chris, Chris, Chrissss!"

"I love the way you say my name," Chris says. Izzie says some indecipherable gibberish. "What was that, my love?"

"Chris, I'm so sorry," Izzie cries out in pleasure.

"Sorry for what?"

"I don't know. You feel so good, I want to apologize for something I didn't even do. I'd confess to murder right now."

Chris laughs and increases his speed. Izzie pussy

clutches around him. "Oh, oh shit. Izzie your pussy..." Chris ends his sentence with some gobbledygook of his own.

Soon the two lovers are moaning nonsense to one other, but the message is very clear. They're both in heaven. The sounds of their moans along with macaroni stirring is enough to send him over the edge, but he waits till Izzie gets hers, she has to get hers first. Always.

"Chris, I gonna come!"

Oh, thank God! Chris pounds her harder.

"Ugh, shiiiitt!" Izzie comes followed by Chris.

"Fuck! Fuck! Fuck!"

They both collapse in a daze.

Minutes later, Chris unties her, and gets some oil from the bathroom before coming back and rubbing her wrists and arms followed by the rest of her body. Touching Izzie's soft supple flesh feels too good to be real. The fact that this impossibly beautiful woman not only allows him to be in her presence, but to put his hands on her, makes his head swim. The oil he's using gives her a floral scent with a hint of citrus. He needs a taste. Running his tongue along the back of her thighs makes her let out a gentle moan and squirm. He licks her some more. Her moans are nothing short of orgasmic. There isn't a single sound more pleasing to the ear. His dick jumps, responding to her sensual siren calls.

Relax, I'm supposed to be taking care of her right now. You just got taken care of.

He rubs her ass cheeks making them clench. Chris gives her a little tap, making them loosen as she yelps.

"Don't tense, Sunflower."

"Sorry, Tiger. It feels so good I'm almost couldn't take it."

"I know the feeling, and I'm glad you're enjoying this because I'm not done with you."

"I can't wait to see what you have in store for me next."

All I can tell is that you'll love it."

"I'm sure I will."

CHRIS IS OILING IZZIE'S SCALP WHILE THEY WATCH *THE Devil Wears Prada.* Yes, it's less sexy than a sensual massage and licking her thighs, but he was right. She loved it. She jumped up and down as he put on the movie and pulled out a comb, a towel and the oil.

He's on the couch while she sits on the floor with the towel around her shoulders. He parts her tresses before adding the oil—Taylor Made of course—to her exposed scalp. Chris basks in the soft moans he elicits from her.

He finishes the left part of her head before working on the right. As he runs the comb through her silky locs, a strange thought pops into his head.

"Iz?"

"Yeah."

"Can you pause the movie?"

"Sure, is everything okay?"

"I'm just stuck on something Blake said."

"Chris don't give that asshole's words a second thought. He'll get his when we take Rossmore Wineries away from him."

"This actually has to do with that."

She turns to look at him. "I'm listening."

"When Michaela mentioned the idea of Parker leaving her everything it made me think of something Blake said. He said grandpa left me everything."

"Maybe he was talking about the sizable amount of money Grandpa Sam left you."

"Then why not just say that? Why say he left me everything? At the time of Grandpa's death, I was too devastated to think straight. Couple that with me still being on relatively good terms with Blake, and it's no wonder why I didn't question him remaining CEO. But given everything that's happened, I think you and I should make a visit to my grandpa's estate lawyer."

"Sounds like a plan."

16

CHRISTOPHER

Chris and Izzie sit in Colden Bridge's office. He was Sam Rossmore's attorney for over thirty years.

"Chris, I haven't seen you since the funeral. How have you been?"

"Doing much better."

"I'm glad, and I'm glad you called this morning."

"I hope it wasn't an inconvenience to rearrange your schedule to see me."

"Not at all. I've been meaning to call you, but I wanted to give you some space. I know how much Sam meant to you. I figured the business was the last thing you'd want to discuss."

"What about the business did *you* want to discuss?"

"You know, signing over the CEO title and ownership of the wineries to you," Colden replies.

Chris and Izzie exchange surprised looks. "Signing over the who and the what now?" *Did I hear him correctly?* "Grandpa left that to my dad. I'm just here to figure out if there's a way I can buy him out."

"You don't need to. When Sam was sick and had to step down, he appointed Blake believing he could handle things temporarily, but your grandfather wasn't a foolish man, Chris. It's why he still held a majority stake in the company, and made a stipulation in his living trust that upon the moment of his death everything would revert to you. You were his backup plan. Blake was never meant to have a permanent place."

That worthless piece of shit. I should have let Izzie kill him.

"Okay, so what do I have to do?"

"Sign a few pieces of paperwork and everything is yours," Colden says.

"Did my father know about this?" Chris asks, already knowing the answer.

"He did. He told me that you would come in to discuss everything when you were ready. That was after the funeral. He contacted me recently about making some changes, he wasn't specific, but he made it seem like you still weren't ready."

"He was just buying time. Probably was going to try and convince me to sign something so he could stay in charge and have Trinese as a figure head." Chris shakes his head in disbelief. He knew his father hated him, but to steal Rossmore Wineries right under his nose was flat on betrayal.

"Your father is a fucking supervillain," Izzie snarls, her lips nearly curling to her nose.

"And not a very good one at that. If he hadn't gone off on me and had just made me CEO, I probably would have agreed to some kind of partnership with him," Chris replies, "but he insisted on making Trinese CEO. That and his angry confession are why I'm here."

"Wait, Trinese? That name sounds familiar." Colden realizes who she is. "You mean the flight attendant?"

"Yep! The bastard made Chris and that heffa compete for the CEO position only to take it away from Chris and give it to her," Izzie explains.

"In that case, let's get these papers signed and get you your title," Colden smiles.

"Let's do it," Chris agrees, grinning from ear to ear.

Even though he grew up in a family of privilege, it still amazes Chris how quickly things move when you have money.

Before the ink could dry on the paperwork, he found himself meeting with the board of directors and the stockholders of Rossmore—this board being remarkably more flexible than the one for Taylor Made—and the majority voted to eject Blake from his current position and appoint Chris as the new CEO. In hindsight, Chris should have had more faith in the people around him. Yes, a few of the board members are golf buddies with his father and would have voted to make Trinese CEO, but the majority were friends of his grandfather's and wouldn't have been foolish enough to destroy his legacy. Samuel Rossmore meant a lot to a lot of people. This situation was a great reminder of that.

TODAY IS THE DAY. CHRIS IS GOING TO RELIEVE HIS father of his duties. Partially nervous and partially ecstatic, Chris holds Izzie's hand as they sit in the back seat with Henri in the driver's seat.

"Thank you again for driving, Henri."

"No problem, Izzie. Today's a big day for Chris."

"Thanks, Henri," Chris adds.

"I have a surprise for you," Izzie says. "I know they aren't official, but I wanted to get you something to commemorate this day."

Izzie pulls out a platinum business card holder and hands it to Chris. When he opens it, there's a small stack of egg-shell-white colored cards with embossed lettering in dark business style font.

CHRISTOPHER S. ROSSMORE

OWNER/CEO ROSSMORE WINERIES AND VINEYARDS

A bubble forms in Chris's throat. It's really happening and no thanks to the man he called father. He gives Izzie a kiss, this means more this she'll ever know. Just then her phone buzzes, she kisses him again before checking the screen.

"I have another surprise for you," Izzie says as she hops out the car.

Chris looks at Henri. "Any ideas?"

"It will be something you'll love," Henri says smiling.

A car pulls up blasting *Move Bitch* by Ludacris and Chris starts laughing. The car parks and out comes Freddie, Artie, and Heather. They each run over and hug Chris.

"What are you all doing here?" Chris smiles.

"You honestly thought we were going to miss this?" Freddie asks.

"You all better be ready to do this again when I have my meeting with the board," Izzie says.

"Of course," Heather says. "We're still trying to work out which song to use."

"Can I make suggestions?" Izzie asks.

"No, goofy, that defeats the whole purpose," Heather answers.

Izzie rolls her eyes prompting the men to laugh at them.

"You ready?" Artie asks Chris.

"I am. Let's go."

The five friends walk into the building and head straight to the elevators heading to the top floor. When they get off, Chris leads them straight to his new office.

He burst through the door while Blake and Trinese were meeting with a group of potential vendors. How did Chris know about this meeting? Because he set it up. Chris did such a superb job booking the Senator's anniversary party that his father gave him the task of finding some potential vendors to partner with. And now here he is running the meeting Chris was responsible for.

"Christopher, what a surprise!" Blake says, trying his best to sound like a doting father.

"When you started working from home, I got concerned."

Ever since they last spoke, Chris found himself going over every conversation he had with his father during the years they were supposed to be bonding. Now that everything is out in the air, he wondered if there were any red flags he missed. But there weren't. Blake was just really good at pretending as though he cared, and that's what hurts the most. His father made him believe he actually loved him… and now he has to pay.

"Blake, you should be receiving an email soon relieving you of your duties as CEO of Rossmore Wineries and Vineyards. I have already spoken with Colden and the paperwork has been signed. A vote was taken, and the majority voted for you to step down and for me to take my rightful place as CEO. Go ahead, check your email."

A stunned expression courses over Blake's flat face. Immediately he takes out his phone and checks his email. Needless to say, it was a treat to watch his face drop as he took in that he was in fact to step down immediately. With wide eyes Blake meets Chris' glare, he almost appears impressed.

"That's not all. Effective immediately you are here by banned from setting foot on any Rossmore property for the rest of your natural life." Chris looks at Trinese. "You too are also banned. And I think this goes without saying, but you obviously don't have a job here."

Blake addresses the vendors. "Would you all please excuse us? I need to talk to my son."

"No, you don't," Chris replies. "And you're right, I'm not your son. I am Samuel Rossmore's. Now gather your belongings and remove yourself from the property or I will have security do it. They're already waiting for my command."

Blake stands still for few moments before finally admitting defeat. He grabs his briefcase and tries to take Trinese's hand, but she snatches it away.

"So, what, that's it? We lose?" she asks.

"Trinese, come on. Don't make a scene," Blake orders.

"Fuck you! You said I was going to get my own private jet. You made me cozy up to that bitch and didn't do anything when she yelled at me. I want my jet, Blake." Trinese's eyes widen like she just realized something. "Oh, my God. You don't have a job anymore. How are we supposed to afford our house, our cars? All our upcoming vacations?"

Chris sends a text to his phone informing security they are needed and not a moment too soon as Trinese directs her ire at Chris.

"You, asshole! You just had to ruin everything! We had it all and you were jealous!"

Amused, Chris lets a smirk spread across his face. "Actually, Trinese—"

"Fuck you, bitch!" Izzie belts out jumping in Trinese's face.

"Back off, Izzie. With your cheap fake ass saggy titties," Trinese spits.

Oh, hell no!

"Go to hell! My titties are not fake and even if they were they'd be top of the line titties because unlike you, I'm not broke," Izzie snaps back.

"That's right!" Chris backs her up. "And there isn't anything saggy about them."

Security enters immediately grabbing Blake and Trinese. Trinese tries to wriggle out of their grip, but it's no use as they escort she and Blake toward the door.

"Wait," Blake says just as they are about to cross

the meeting room's threshold. He looks at Chris with an earnest expression. His eyes soft and his brows relaxed. "This might be the first time I've actually been proud of you."

Chris takes in his words and feels… nothing. No sense of pride, no desire to be praised again. Nothing. He's finally free.

"I don't give a fuck. Get out," Chris replies.

"And Blake," Izzie adds. Blake turns to her. "If you ever try to cozy up to Chris again, don't let the pretty face, and curvy figure fool you." Izzie's eyes turn dark and cold. "I will kill you."

This must've stunned Blake. His Adam's apple bobbed so hard you'd think he nearly swallowed his own tongue.

Security escorts him and Trinese off the property. Chris apologizes to the vendors promising to follow up with them next week. One even pats him on the back and congratulates Chris, saying it was one of the more interesting meetings they had ever attended.

Once the vendors exit the office, the friends celebrate with a bottle of champagne.

"I know one thing. This office needs an upgrade. Chris, that should be the first thing you do." Heather suggests.

"That's definitely on my to do list. It feels like a fucking coffin in here," Chris replies.

"Okay so this has been fun, but I want to congratulate Chris alone," Izzie announces.

"Wow, so you're just going to kick us out so you two can fuck?" Artie says.

"Yeah, pretty much," Izzie answers.

"Okay, well don't fuck each other into a coma. We're meeting for Chris' celebration dinner, remember?" Freddie says.

"We'll be there," Izzie assures him.

Artie and Freddie leave together with Artie whispering something to Fred that made him chuckle. Meanwhile, Heather stays where she is, sitting across from the large desk Chris and Izzie are leaning on.

"I'm gonna stay and watch," Heather declares.

"No, you aren't," Chris says.

"What the hell is wrong with you?" Izzie replies chuckling.

Heather rolls her eyes and gets up. "You two are such prudes. I was going to send you both an invite to Decadence as a congratulatory gift, but now I think I'll do it because you both could stand to loosen up a bit. Ciao."

Izzie and Chris chuckle at their friend before gazing at each other.

"So, you want to fuck on the desk?" Izzie asks.

"Yep."

Chris throws everything off the desk and picks up Izzie laying her down. She giggles the whole time.

17

ISOBEL

The lobby of Taylor Made offices is quiet. It could be nerves or simply the lack of human occupancy in the area, no matter the case, Chris and Izzie wait patiently. Izzie wanted to get there extra early. She takes deep breaths and thinks about all the updates and changes she wants to bring to the table. Even though she's confident in the outcome, she could really use some theme music right now to get her hyped.

"Where's the crew? You got theme music. I thought I was getting some too," Izzie complains.

"You are. They're saving your celebration music for after the meeting," Chris replies.

"I guess."

Chris smiles at her and takes out his phone and presses play. "Suddenly I see" by KT Tunstall floats through the air. "There you go. Channel your inner Miranda Priestly."

"Funny you should say that." Izzie beams and gives him a kiss.

A half hour later, Izzie sits among the board while they show more footage from Izzie and Chris' relationship. It's interviews done by TRNN of the alleged witnesses who saw Chris go off on the photographer. It's like they brought up anything they could to throw in Izzie's face, because why does this even matter?

Gordon Petrie stops the footage and nods for the assistant to turn on the lights. "Isobel, can you explain this?" Gordon looks at her with contempt. His eyes narrowed and his brows knit.

It really doesn't matter how qualified Izzie is, this man will always try to make her look and feel small. She can't believe she let this nonsense get to her. Well, no more.

"Sure, I can. TRNN hires the same people repeatedly to say that they witnessed things they didn't actually see. If you look up a recent story they did on singer Chantel Stone and actor Robert Emerson, you'll see that the woman who first spoke was also a witness for the Stone and Emerson encounter. What are the chances that this same woman witnessed two different occurrences around the same time?" Izzie inquires. Gordon doesn't respond so Izzie continues. "People of the board. My party girl antics—as you call them—have afforded me the advantage of building relationships."

Now it's Izzie's turn to nod at the assistant. They get up and log on to Zoom permitting everyone waiting to enter. There are numerous screens of people who are on the call including Michaela.

"It is through these relationships that I have made deals to assist Taylor Made well into the future. These wonderful folks who are joining us have made deals with me including Dottie Kane, owner of the Beautiful Bust Downs Wig Shops and Salons. Hi, Dottie."

"Hello, Isobel."

"Dottie is going to team up with Taylor Made so we can start selling our wigs exclusively in her shops. I am also in talks with Coopersmith labs to start Taylor Made's new make-up line. And last but not least, Taylor Made is going to be the official haircare for Michaela Hamilton and Hunter Lawrence's upcoming new reality show."

"You are in no position to make those deals, Isobel," Gordon argues.

"Am I not? I am an employee of Taylor Made. I have already shown my projected figures to my father. He's in agreement. You all are the only hold-outs. Also, I would like to add that if you still aren't inclined to make me CEO, all these lovely people joining us have promised me that they will follow me whenever and if ever I decide to leave Taylor Made."

"Did you just quote *The Devil Wears Prada?*" Sylvia asks.

"Damn right, I did. Think about it, friends. That's billions of dollars in revenue staring back at you. All of whom are ready to come with me."

The board shifts their focus on Gordon. He's toast and he knows it. Gordon clears his throat looking sheepish as if he's finally ready to admit defeat.

"All in favor of Isobel Taylor being named CEO of Taylor Made Haircare. Say aye," Gordon says.

Everyone says, "Aye."

"All opposed?" The room is so quiet you could hear a wig fall. "The 'ayes' have it." Gordon turns to Izzie. "Congratulations, Isobel. You're Taylor Made's new CEO."

"Thank you," Izzie says, releasing the air from her lungs. Everyone on the screen claps and cheers, and Izzie's smile is a mile wide. "The Savage Remix" by Megan Thee Stallion and Beyonce plays at top volume. Without restraint, Izzie runs out of the board room and jumps into the arms of her friends.

"Congratulations, Ms. CEO!" Heather yells. Artie and Freddie cheer.

Izzie leaps right into Chris' arms. He kisses her before pulling her back.

"I did it, Chris! Taylor Made is mine," Izzie cries.

"Of course you did. You're a baddie!" Chris kisses her again.

LATER THAT NIGHT CHRIS AND IZZIE TAKE HEATHER up on her invite to Decadence. It's an exclusive sex club for the rich that offers the privacy to indulge in every kink imaginable. Nothing illegal, of course. Heather and Artie have been members for years and agreed they would get Chris and Izzie to join once they got their heads out of their asses.

When Chris asked Izzie how she wanted to cele-brate she could tell he was talking in terms of taking a trip or going to dinner. When she said she wanted to experience Decadence, he was pleased and got on the phone with Heather right away.

This club is elaborate and sexy. Izzie is taken aback, but exhilarated. Seeing a throuple engage in public sex the minute they walked in was not on her bingo card but she's here to celebrate and have fun. Besides, playing with Chris in this type of environment will make both of them come endlessly. She can't wait.

Heather approaches them after smacking a man with a movie star smile and leather assless chaps on his butt. "Hey kids! Are you having fun?" she asks.

"We're about to, once we get a private room." Chris squeezes Izzie close.

"No problem. Just talk to the concierge." Heather looks around. "I'm on the hunt for a new sub, wish me luck."

"Good luck." They both say as Heather makes her way into the crowd.

After acquiring a room, the concierge leads Izzie and Chris to the *Pillow Talk* room, named after the Rock Hudson and Doris Day movie of the same name.

Chris takes a seat on the bed. He's wearing one of his signature business suits and looks fine as hell. Powerful even.

Izzie has on red lace lingerie under her trench coat. There were people walking around naked, but Izzie isn't there yet. She drops her coat and bites her lip as Chris looks her up and down. Finally, he pats his lap encouraging Izzie to take a seat.

As soon as her soft bottom hits his thigh, Chris runs his hands all over her body. "Goddamn," he mutters.

"What would you like to do first?" Izzie asks.

"So many things, I'm not sure where to start."

Izzie teeters in front of Chris and takes off everything. As she stands before him naked his eyes darken. He checks the drawers and finds toys, ropes, whips, and chains are all available to them. He of course chooses the ropes. He gestures with his finger for Izzie to come to him then pats the bed. Izzie climbs on the bed and Chris proceeds to hogtie her.

"Are you comfortable?" Chris asks.

"Yes," Izzie answers.

"Good."

Chris stands in front of the bed and removes all of his clothes. He turns Izzie onto her stomach and moves her to the foot of the bed before retaking his spot. His dick brushes against Izzie's lips teasing them both. Izzie kisses one of Chris' veins making his dick pulsate. She traces the vein with the tip of her tongue.

"Fuck, Izzie."

Izzie takes Chris dick into her mouth and moans, loving how his veins feel against her tongue. This thick, long dick is one of Izzie's top two cravings and it ain't number two. Chris pushes his dick in and out of her mouth. She tickles the tip with her tongue making him shake and quiver.

"Oh, shit, Sunflower. Be careful. I just might bust all over your face." This spurs Izzie to give him more tickles and faster. She then sucks on his head. "Ugh! Shit," Chris groans.

"Mmmmm." Izzie takes more of his dick in her mouth. He thrust in and out again fucking her mouth.

"Oh, your mouth is so wet and warm, Iz. I'm going to come down your throat. You want that Sunflower? You want this hot ass load going down your throat?"

Izzie nods and says a muffled, "mmmhmmm."

With each thrust, Izzie bobs her head meeting his hips. Drool slides down her chin. She backs away and spits on his dick then licks it up before going back in.

"Iz, Iz, Iz. Ah!" Chris screams as he unloads in her mouth.

Izzie breathes carefully and swallows sucking any leftover come down her throat. She keeps sucking, she just can't stop. Chris' dick feels too good. Chris lets out some gibberish this time in a high-pitched voice before he pulls out and stumbles onto the bed.

"Chris." Izzie calls for him, but he's knocked out.

She looks at him and tries to wiggle herself free.

"Chris," she calls out again. Still nothing. "Oh, you have got to be kidding me." She says. Izzie wiggles some more before she hears chuckles. Chris appears in front of her, face to face. "You asshole." Izzie laughs.

"Watch your mouth, Sunflower."

"Sorry, but that was a dirty trick. Could you please untie me now?"

"Sure." Chris chuckles some more.

Minutes later they lay in bed as Chris rubs oil on Izzie's ankle and massages it along with her foot. "This is heaven." Izzie sighs.

"It is, isn't it?" Chris kisses her ankle.

"Now that we have our dream jobs and each other, where do we go from here?" Izzie asks.

"Wherever we want. So how about it, where do you want to be most in the world, Iz?"

"Your arms, Tiger. I want to be in your arms."

Chris places her foot down and gathers her in his arms holding her close. "And that's where you'll always be," Chris says, planting a soft kiss on her lips.

THE END

ACKNOWLEDGMENTS

I would like to thank Lucy Eden and Hellhoney for the amazing cover! Randi Love for her excellent beta reading and proofreading skills. Editor extraordinaire Jaz Wilson, this is our second collaboration and it won't be our last. Copy editor Ms. Brianna, this was my first time working with her and I highly recommend her! Lily Flowers for making sure the BDSM scenes were accurate and sexy and last but not least my girl Ms. Brynn for her formatting talents.

I would also like to give a shout out to all the amazing reading and writing friends that I have made along this journey.

I hope you all enjoyed this book. It was probably my toughest book to write but also so much fun. Please be on the look out next year for Heather's story "Make Room for Heather" coming in 2025!! Smooches 🤍